SARAH, PLAIN AND TALL

A Play in Two Acts

Based on the book by
Patricia MacLachlan

Adapted for the stage by
Joseph Robinette

Dramatic Publishing
Woodstock, Illinois • England • Australia • New Zealand

*** NOTICE ***

©MMIII by
Joseph Robinette
Based on the novel by
Patricia MacLachlan

Printed in the United States of America
All Rights Reserved
(SARAH, PLAIN AND TALL)

ISBN 1-58342-161-0

IMPORTANT BILLING AND CREDIT REQUIREMENTS

All producers of the play *must* give credit to the author(s) of the play in all programs distributed in connection with performances of the play and in all instances in which the title of the play appears for purposes of advertising, publicizing or otherwise exploiting the play and/or a production. The name of the author(s) *must* also appear on a separate line, on which no other name appears, immediately following the title, and *must* appear in size of type not less than fifty percent the size of the title type. Biographical information on the author(s), if included in this book, may be used on all programs. *On all programs this notice must appear:*

SARAH, PLAIN AND TALL

A Play in Two Acts
For 5 Men and 7 Women*
(And up to 6 additional Men and/or Women, if desired)

MAJOR CHARACTERS

Jacob Witting . . . . a Kansas farmer
Anna Witting . . . . his young daughter
Caleb Witting . . . . his young son
Matthew Nordstrom . . . . a neighboring farmer
Maggie Nordstrom . . . . his wife
Rose Nordstrom . . . . their daughter
Violet Nordstrom . . . . their other daughter
William Wheaton . . . . a Maine fisherman
Meg Wheaton . . . . his wife
Sarah Wheaton . . . . his sister
Adult Anna . . . . Anna Witting in her 20s

(The 4 children's roles may be played by children, juveniles or
even youthful-appearing adults)

MINOR CHARACTERS

Ephraim (Eppie) . . . . a paperboy
Howie (Hettie) . . . . a postman
Eben (Esther) . . . . a coachman
Levi (Laurey) . . . . a stationmaster
Mr. (Miss) Titus . . . . a farmer
Chester (Hester) Upshaw . . . . a salesman
Judson Moffet . . . . a neighbor of the Wittings

(All minor characters may be played by 1 Man, or by as many
as 1 Man and 6 Men and/or Women)

THE TIME: The early 1900s.
THE PLACE: A farm in Kansas / a house in Maine.

*May be performed by a cast of 10—see production notes for
doubling.

ACT ONE

(The stage is in semi-darkness. The offstage VOICE of ADULT ANNA, early to mid-twenties, is heard singing "Nature's Song."*)

ADULT ANNA.
>WHEN A TREE GROWS, IT GROWS.
>WHEN THE WIND BLOWS, IT BLOWS.
>THAT'S THE WAY THEY WERE MADE,
>LET THEM BE.

(She continues to sing or hum. She enters wearing every-day clothing, but holding a fancy hat. She moves slowly DRC toward a pool of light.)

>WHEN A BIRD TWEETS A TUNE
>AND A WOLF HOWLS THE MOON,
>THAT'S THE WAY THEY WERE MADE,
>NATURALLY.

(She hums a few more notes, then her voice trails off as she puts the hat on and mimes looking at herself in an unseen mirror.)

---

* See production notes for complete lyrics and melody lines for the four songs sung a cappella in the play.

ADULT ANNA. Oh, it's lovely. Maybe one or two more ribbons down the back, then it will be just right.

JACOB'S VOICE *(from offstage)*. How does the hat look in the *big* mirror, Anna?

ADULT ANNA *(calling to offstage)*. Just fine, Papa. Maybe another ribbon or two, and it'll be perfect.

JACOB'S VOICE. You know—the roses have just come in. I'll bet a few of those might brighten it up.

ADULT ANNA *(to offstage)*. Oh, yes. Maybe two or three on the brim when she gets back from town. *(Adjusting the hat, calling back to offstage.)* You know, this hat is going to look so nice, I may not wear anything on Saturday except this and a pair of old comfortable overalls. *(She laughs, joined by JACOB's offstage laughter. Overlapping their voices is the offstage laughter of four CHILDREN. To herself:)* What was that? It sounded like children laughing. *(She listens intently, then shrugs.)* I must be hearing things. *(To the audience for the first time.)* Papa said the next few days might be pretty unusual for me—that I'd probably be having a lot of memories of the past. That happens, he says, when people are getting ready for a big change in their lives—like leaving home, taking their first job, going on an adventure. Why, just yesterday I was remembering the first automobile I ever saw. That was about ten years ago when a man from Topeka came by and tried to sell Papa some shingles. Then last night I started thinking about the— *(The offstage CHILDREN's laughter is heard again.)* Who *was* that?

ANNA'S VOICE *(from offstage)*. Coming, ready or not! *(More CHILDREN's laughter.)*

ADULT ANNA. That was *me* ... Papa was right. I *am* going to be remembering a lot of things over the next few days.

(She slowly moves R as the pool of light crossfades with the general lighting which comes up to reveal an open space outside the Witting farmhouse. A rustic table and three or four chairs and/or upside down barrels are at C. A basket of unfolded laundry is on the table.

At extreme R is a small platform containing two chairs and a table which serve as the Wheaton parlor throughout the play. That area is lit only for the scenes played in Maine. A similar platform containing a water pump, corn grinder or other farm implement may be located at extreme L to serve as balance.

Four entrances are suggested. UL leads to the farmhouse. DL goes to other areas of the farm and to the road. UR leads to the barn, cow pond and fields. DR, below the parlor, is used for entrances to the Wheaton home and the railway station in Kansas. NOTE: a door, real or imagined, is at the rear of the parlor, leading to the rest of the house—an imaginary door, going to the outside, is at the front of the parlor.

During the lighting change, three children, ROSE, VIO-LET and CALEB, enter running from DL, laughing and calling to offstage behind them, "Can't find me!" "I know where I'm going to hide!" "You'll never spy me, Anna!" Etc. They exit offstage UR or UR and UL.)

ADULT ANNA. That's Caleb, my little brother. The girls are Rose and Violet Nordstrom, our next-door neighbors. I say next door. They lived two miles away. But in these parts that was pretty close.

(ANNA enters from DL running, then stops.)

ADULT ANNA. And there *I* am.

ANNA *(creeps about the stage, then calls out)*. I spy Rose behind the trellis.

ROSE'S VOICE. Oh, no.

ANNA. I spy Caleb next to the rain barrel.

CALEB. Oh, shoot.

ANNA. And I spy—Violet under the fence.

VIOLET'S VOICE. Oh, phooey.

(ROSE, CALEB and VIOLET slowly emerge from their hiding places and come toward C.)

ANNA. I told you I'd find you. Rose, I saw you first, so you're it this time.

CALEB. Close your eyes and count to twenty while we hide.

ROSE. Okay. Ready—set—go! *(ANNA, VIOLET and CALEB exit at UR, laughing as ROSE counts.)* One, two, three, four, five, six, seven, eight, nine, ten. *(She opens one eye, then looks up and around and whispers.)* Fif- teen. *(Opening both eyes and shouting.)* Twenty! Com- ing, ready or not! *(She exits giggling.)*

ADULT ANNA. Rose and Violet were my best friends— practically my *only* friends in the summer when we weren't in school. Their parents were Matthew and Mag- gie. Sometimes they would help Papa with the plowing or a big crop gathering. And we would help *them*, too. We worked hard, but they let us children play from time to time to keep from getting too tired or too bored.

ROSE'S VOICE *(from offstage)*. I spy Caleb!... I spy Violet!... But I don't see Anna!

ADULT ANNA *(going UR and looking offstage)*. Where was I?... Oh, yes. I remember.

ROSE'S VOICE. Anna, where are you hiding? Anna!

ADULT ANNA. Under the big haystack next to the barn.

(She exits as JACOB, mid-thirties, and MATTHEW and MAGGIE, early forties and late thirties respectively, enter from DL.)

JACOB. Thank you, Matthew. Much obliged, Maggie. I could never have cleared off those four acres without you.

MATTHEW. You're more than welcome, Jacob.

MAGGIE. You always give us a hand when you can.

JACOB. But I get *two* of you. There's only one of me. *(Offstage laughter as the parents smile.)* Anna and Caleb sure are crazy about Rose and Violet. They'll be bored stiff when you leave. And they're getting too big for me to entertain—especially when I'm working most of the day.

MATTHEW. Well, Jacob, you need to get yourself some help—just like I did. *(He puts his arm around MAGGIE's waist.)*

JACOB. I might not be as lucky as you were, Matthew.

MATTHEW. You never can tell unless you try... I was a little nervous myself at first, but there I was—my dear wife passed away and me left with two little girls. So, I put an advertisement in the newspapers. Then one day I got a letter from Tennessee. And three months later I was married to this wonderful woman.

JACOB. But what if I advertised, and the person who answered didn't get along with me?

MAGGIE. You don't get married right away. When I came to Matthew and the girls, they gave me my own room. In the meantime we got to know each other—and we all liked what we saw.

MATTHEW. I told Rose and Violet all three of us had to agree on Maggie. *And*, of course, she had to agree on us.

JACOB. How do you know which papers to advertise in?

MATTHEW. Get a list from Editor Price in town. He's got the names of every paper in all forty-six states. Pick a few and send them your advertisement. Doesn't cost that much.

JACOB. What do you say in an advertisement like that?

MATTHEW. You can say exactly what I said— "Tall, handsome farmer. Very smart. Went all the way to the eighth grade. Has two children. Seeks a wife."

JACOB. Tall? Handsome? Smart? Did you believe that, Maggie?

MAGGIE. 'Course not. I figured if he was all that, he wouldn't need to advertise for a wife. (*They laugh.*) Anyway, I decided any man who'd tell tales like that shouldn't be raising two little children all by himself. (*More laughter.*)

MATTHEW (*becoming serious*). You think about that advertisement, Jacob. It's one of the best things I ever did.

JACOB. I *will* think about it. But if I do write one up, I'll just tell the truth about myself. When you tell the truth you never have to remember what you said. It always comes out the same every time.

(The CHILDREN enter from UR, laughing and exchanging friendly barbs— "You never did spy me," "Did, too," "I know you didn't count up to twenty," "I was 'it' only one time." Etc.)

MAGGIE. Come on, girls. Time to go home.

MATTHEW. Who wants to help me hitch up the horses to the wagon?

ROSE & VIOLET. Me! Me! Me, please! Etc.

MATTHEW. Okay, you can both help. *(ROSE and VIOLET cheer.)*

ANNA. Do you have to go now?

MAGGIE. 'Fraid so, Anna. We still have *our* chores to do.

MATTHEW. Cows to be milked.

MAGGIE. Supper to be made.

JACOB. Thank you again, Matthew—Maggie. And you, too, Rose and Violet. You were a big help.

ROSE. You're welcome.

VIOLET. You're welcome.

JACOB. We'll be over next Tuesday to help you clean out the chicken houses and put down some new straw.

MATTHEW. We'll look forward to it. *(MATTHEW, MAGGIE, ROSE and VIOLET begin to leave.)*

ANNA. 'Bye, Rose.

CALEB. 'Bye, Violet.

ROSE & VIOLET. 'Bye.

MAGGIE. Girls, on the way home I'll tell you the story about Davy Crockett and his coonskin cap.

ROSE. And tell us the one about Daniel Boone again. *(MAGGIE, ROSE and VIOLET exit DL.)*

MATTHEW *(to JACOB)*. They love those stories about Tennessee. It's almost like hearing about a foreign country ... You think about that newspaper advertisement, Jacob. *(He exits DL.)*

JACOB *(calling after MATTHEW)*. I will. See you on Tuesday. *(A pause as he, ANNA and CALEB watch the family depart.)*

ANNA. Rose calls Maggie "Mama."

CALEB. Violet does, too.

ANNA. But Maggie's not their real mama.

CALEB. Is, too.

ANNA. Is not.

CALEB. Is, too.

ANNA. Is not.

JACOB. That's enough, children. Now you two fold the laundry over there. I'll be in the parlor. We'll have an early supper tonight. I need to be up at the crack of dawn to go into town on an errand.

CALEB. Can I help you hitch Jack up to the wagon?

ANNA. Jack won't let anybody but Papa hitch him up. He's too feisty.

JACOB. I'll be gone before you're up. I'll leave food in a skillet on the wood stove. After breakfast, be sure you do your chores.

ANNA. Okay, Papa.

CALEB. Okay, Papa. *(JACOB exits UL as ANNA and CALEB begin to fold the laundry.)* Rose and Violet are lucky. They have somebody to tell them stories. I wish Papa would tell us stories.

ANNA. He's too tired from working all day. He doesn't even sing anymore.

CALEB. Did Mama sing every day? Every—single—day?

ANNA. Every—single—day. That's the second time I told you this week. The twentieth time this month. The hundredth time this year.

CALEB. And did Papa sing, too?

ANNA. Yes. Papa sang, too... Fold those things a little straighter, Caleb.

CALEB. Papa doesn't sing anymore.

ANNA. No. He doesn't. *(A pause as they fold.)*

CALEB. What did I look like when I was born?

ANNA. You didn't have any clothes on.

CALEB. I know that.

ANNA. You looked like a round ball of bread dough.

CALEB. I had hair.

ANNA. Not enough to talk about.

CALEB *(as though continuing a story)*. And she named me Caleb.

ANNA. I would have named you Troublesome.

CALEB. And Mama handed me to you in the yellow blanket and said... *(Waiting for ANNA to finish the story.)* And said...?

ANNA *(with a sigh)*. And Mama said, "Isn't he beautiful, Anna?"

CALEB. And I was.

(They continue folding the laundry in silence as ADULT ANNA enters.)

ADULT ANNA. Caleb thought the story was over, and I didn't tell him what I really thought—that he was homely and plain, and he had a terrible holler and a horrid smell. But these were not the worst of him. Mama died the next morning. That was the worst thing about Caleb.

CALEB *(dreamily, to himself)*. "Isn't he beautiful, Anna?"

ADULT ANNA. Those were her last words to me. I had gone to bed thinking how wretched he looked. And I forgot to say good night.

CALEB. Can you remember her songs? Mama's songs?

ANNA. No. Only that she sang about flowers and birds. Sometimes about the moon at nighttime. *(They have finished folding the laundry.)* Let's go. We need to put these things away. *(She has sorted the folded laundry into two stacks, one of which she gives to CALEB.)* You put these in our room, and I'll take the rest to Papa's room.

CALEB. Okay. *(As they leave.)* Anna, maybe if you remember her songs, then I might remember her, too. *(They exit UL.)*

ADULT ANNA. In my heart I had forgiven Caleb. I knew it was not his fault that Mama had died. But I hadn't forgiven myself for not saying good night to her. The truth is, on that particular night I hadn't wanted to. It would be a long time before I got over it.

(JACOB enters from DL carrying a newspaper.)

JACOB. Children!

ADULT ANNA. A week or so after the Nordstroms were at the farm, Papa called Caleb and me together for an important announcement. *(She exits.)*

JACOB. Anna, Caleb. Gather 'round. I have something to tell you.

(ANNA and CALEB enter from UL.)

ANNA. Yes, Papa?

CALEB. What is it, Papa?

JACOB. I've placed an advertisement in several newspapers. For help.

ANNA. You mean a housekeeper?

CALEB. Like old Hilly? *(He and ANNA laugh.)*

ANNA. She always snored at night—like a teakettle.

CALEB. And she always let the fire go out.

JACOB. No. Not a housekeeper this time... A wife.

CALEB. A wife? You mean a mother?

JACOB. That, too. Like Maggie.

ANNA. But—but we don't need a mother.

CALEB. I'd like to have a mother.

ANNA. *I* can cook and do the laundry and lots of other chores.

JACOB. That's true, Anna. You're very helpful. Caleb, too. But you're both in school much of the time. And there are some things that are better done by grown people.

ANNA. I—I'm practically grown.

JACOB. That will be a few more years yet.

ANNA. I think we're doing pretty well without a mother. Besides, Matthew and Maggie help us out.

JACOB. When they can. But they have their own farm to tend. *(An arm around ANNA.)* But let's not talk about it anymore right now. Okay? Anyway, nobody's answered the advertisement yet. Maybe nobody will. *(He sniffs the air.)* Hmmm. That stew you put on the back porch to cool smells good. *(Sniffing near ANNA's hair.)* Has a nice soapy smell.

ANNA *(smiling)*. Papa, that's my hair.

JACOB. Oh, so it is. *(JACOB takes CALEB's hands and swings him around in a circle. CALEB squeals with delight.)*

CALEB. Papa, will you push us on the swing out back?

JACOB. Sure... You know, if I had somebody to help me, I'd have time to do even more things with both of you. Come on. Let's go swing while the stew cools down. *(Sniffing the air again.) Now* it smells like stew.

(They laugh and exit UL. The lights crossfade to the Wheaton's parlor as EPHRAIM, a paperboy, enters from DR. He goes to the "front door" and calls out.)

EPHRAIM. Evening paper, Mr. Wheaton!

(WILLIAM, late twenties or early thirties, enters the parlor from the rear and goes to the "door.")

WILLIAM *(taking the paper).* Thank you, Ephraim. Mind you don't slip and fall out there. Roads are awful muddy after that squall we had this morning.

EPHRAIM. Yes sir, Mr. Wheaton. *(He exits DR.)*

WILLIAM *(calling out).* Paper, Meg!

(He sits as MEG, mid- to late twenties, enters.)

WILLIAM. Would you like the front section, dear?

MEG. No thank you, darling. I'm not in the mood for bad news and politics today. I'll leave that to you. Maybe I'll just look at the advertising section.

WILLIAM. The advertising section?

MEG. I like to see what people are buying and selling.

WILLIAM. Very well. Here you are. *(He hands her the section. They both read in silence for a moment.)* Hmm. Looks like we may get a new state this year.

MEG *(responding perfunctorily as she reads)*. Another state?

WILLIAM. Ayuh. New Mexico.

MEG *(after a moment)*. Hmm. Here's a small cottage for sale. It's nearby—*and* at a good price.

WILLIAM. What are you talking about, Meg? We have a house. Right here. The one I grew up in.

MEG. I know. But—I was thinking about—Sarah.

WILLIAM. This is her home, too. The one *she* grew up in as well. There's plenty of room here for all of us.

MEG. Oh, William, you know I love Sarah. She's almost like a sister to me. But as long as she lives here, I'll never feel this is truly our home. *My* home.

WILLIAM. I understand, dear. But I could never ask Sarah to leave. And *we* certainly can't live elsewhere. A man who makes his living as a fisherman has to live near the water's edge.

MEG. I know.

WILLIAM. I realize Sarah can be a little headstrong at times.

MEG. And stubborn.

WILLIAM. And independent.

MEG. And unyielding.

WILLIAM. And—that's enough. But asking her to leave is out of the question. At least, not now anyway. *(They go back to their reading.)* Goodness, it says here the president weighs over three hundred pounds. That's heavier than all the fish I catch in a week.

(They are both buried in their papers as SARAH, mid- to late twenties, wearing rubber overalls and a rubber fisherman's hat, enters through the rear door to the parlor. She is holding a large fish from a stringer. She is creep-

*ing up to surprise WILLIAM and MEG but is stopped,
unseen, by their conversation.)*

MEG. William.

WILLIAM. Yes, dear?

MEG. Here's an ad from a man looking for a wife. That
could be the perfect solution.

WILLIAM. Solution for what, dear?

MEG. What we were talking about.

WILLIAM. I'm sorry, Meg. I don't wish to discuss it fur-
ther.

MEG. But what harm could there be in having her write
the gentleman? *(SARAH turns and creeps away, exiting
quietly.)* She's never courted a man before—except for
that fellow you said she met at church. Didn't you say
he proposed marriage?

WILLIAM. I think so.

MEG. Whatever happened?

WILLIAM. I don't know. A falling-out, I guess.

SARAH'S VOICE *(from offstage)*. Hello in there!

WILLIAM. Oh. It's Sarah.

(SARAH enters.)

SARAH. Look what I caught.

MEG. My stars.

WILLIAM. It's a sea bass bigger than anything *I* ever net-
ted. I declare, sister, I think you can do anything a man
can do. *(He takes the fish from SARAH.)*

SARAH. Well, I could do even better if I had a new rowboat. I wonder if somebody might be selling one. Do
either of you have the advertising section?

MEG. I do. *(She hands the paper to SARAH who begins to read.)*

WILLIAM. I think the rowboat we have is perfectly satisfactory.

SARAH *(as she looks at the paper)*. That's because you never use it. You always take the big boat to fish in. *(A pause.)* Wait a minute. What is this?

WILLIAM. You found a boat for sale?

SARAH. No. It's a man who says he's seeking a wife.

MEG *(overly down-playing the idea)*. Well, why on earth would you be interested in something like that?

SARAH. I don't know. Maybe it's time for me to see another part of the country.

WILLIAM. But, Sarah, you don't even know the man.

SARAH. Well, it says here he has two children—that his wife died—he has a small farm—and he lives in Kansas. That's a start.

WILLIAM. But—to be his wife?

SARAH. I wouldn't think of marrying him immediately.

MEG. Of course not. She could go and stay with them for, say—a month.

SARAH. And if things didn't work out, I'd come back.

MEG. Where you would be perfectly welcome, of course. *(Quickly taking a pencil—or pen—and writing paper from the table and handing it to SARAH.)* Now, we'll help you with the letter... "Dear, sir, I am a tall, beautiful woman, and it is plain to see I would be perfect—"

SARAH. Well, I think the tall and plain part may be true. But we'll have to let *him* decide on the beautiful and perfect part.

MEG. Now, now, Sarah, dear. Don't sell yourself short. You want to list all your outstanding qualities, and—

WILLIAM. Meg, darling, I think Sarah is perfectly capable of writing the letter herself.

MEG. Of course she is. I'm just trying to help—

WILLIAM. Let's go check on the chowder. I'll clean the sea bass, and we'll have it for supper as well.

MEG. Certainly, dear. *(She and WILLIAM start to leave.)* Oh, and mention you're handy with tools. I'm sure they have lots of tools in Kansas.

WILLIAM *(gently scolding)*. Meg.

MEG. Of course, dear. The chowder. I'm coming. *(They exit. SARAH emits a sigh, smiles weakly and sits at the table. After a moment, she begins to write.)*

SARAH. "Dear Mr. Jacob Witting, I am Sarah Wheaton from Maine as you will see from my letter. I am answering your advertisement. I have never been married, though I have been asked. I live with my brother and his wife who is young and energetic."

(JACOB, followed by ANNA and CALEB, enters at UL. JACOB is holding an opened letter which he begins reading with SARAH.)

JACOB & SARAH. "I have always loved to live by the sea, but at this time I feel a move is necessary." *(SARAH's voice begins to trail off as she continues writing.)* "I am strong and I work hard and I am willing to travel. But I am not mild mannered."

JACOB. "If you should still care to write, I would be interested in your children and about where you live. And you."

SARAH. "Very truly yours, Sarah Elisabeth Wheaton... P.S. Do you have an opinion on cats? I have one." *(She stands and folds the letter as she exits.)*

JACOB *(after a pause)*. Well, what do you think of that? She says she would be interested in my children... I have a good idea. Let's each of us write her a letter so she can get to know *us* a little better.

CALEB. Yes, Papa. That's a very good idea.

ANNA. Do we have to, Papa?

JACOB. I think it would be a nice thing to do.

ANNA. I don't know what to write.

JACOB. Just tell her something about yourself. And ask her something about *her*self.

CALEB. I'm going to ask her if she snores.

ANNA. Don't you dare. *(JACOB laughs.)*

CALEB. I'll also ask if she sings.

ANNA. Maybe Papa should ask if she sings.

JACOB. We'll write the letters tonight after supper. But right now we have chores to do. *(They start to exit.)*

CALEB. Papa, will you help me spell the words I can't spell?

JACOB. Of course. That is, if *I* can spell them.

(They laugh and exit at DL as HOWIE, a postman, enters from DR.)

HOWIE. Morning, Wheatons! Mail for you today.

(WILLIAM enters the parlor and goes to the "front door.")

WILLIAM. Thank you, Howie.

HOWIE. Three letters and a package.

WILLIAM *(taking the mail and looking at the package)*. Good. Must be the fishhooks I ordered.

HOWIE *(looking skyward)*. Appears to be a good one today.

WILLIAM. Ayuh. The flounder should be close to the shore in weather like this.

HOWIE. Well, good day to you, William.

WILLIAM. And to you as well, Howie.

(HOWIE exits DR as MEG enters.)

MEG *(in a loud whisper)*. Anything from that man in Kansas yet?

WILLIAM *(looking at the letters)*. Not *one* thing.

MEG *(disappointed)*. Gracious.

WILLIAM. But, how about—*three* things?

MEG *(delighted)*. Goodness! *(Calling to offstage.)* Sarah! Sarah! Come quickly! *(She takes the letters from WILLIAM as SARAH enters drying her hands on a dish towel.)* Three letters from Kansas. It looks like one from the father and two from the children. They must really be interested. *(She hands the letters to SARAH.)*

WILLIAM. Or maybe they're just being nosy. Sarah, don't answer any questions you don't want to.

MEG. William, Sarah is a grown woman. She doesn't need us to tell her what to do. *(To SARAH.)* Now, be sure to write each one of them individually. It'll make them feel special. And I wouldn't sign the letters—"*Love*, Sarah Wheaton"—just yet. You don't want to sound too eager. And—

WILLIAM. Meg, darling, I think I just heard someone say Sarah is a grown woman.

MEG. Yes, but—

WILLIAM *(to MEG as he takes the dishtowel from SARAH)*. Come, dear. Let's go into the kitchen and finish the breakfast dishes.

MEG. Very well. *(In a loud whisper to WILLIAM.)* I was just trying to help her chances. That's all.

(She and WILLIAM exit as SARAH opens a letter, smiles and silently reads. A moment later she sits, puts the letter down and begins to write a letter of her own. ANNA enters from DL reading a letter and holding a large envelope.)

ANNA. "Dear Anna, Yes, I can braid hair and I can make stew and bake bread, though I prefer to build bookcases and paint."

(She continues to read, but silently, as CALEB enters from UL reading a letter.)

CALEB. "Dear Caleb, My cat's name is Seal because she is gray like the seals that swim offshore in Maine. She is glad that your dogs, Lottie and Nick, send their greetings. She likes dogs most of the time." *(He reads silently.)*

ANNA *(reading)*. "My brother William catches flounder and sea bass and bluefish. Sometimes he sees whales. And birds, too, of course. I am enclosing a book of sea birds so you will see what we see every day." *(She pulls the book from the envelope and looks at it as CALEB reads.)*

CALEB. "My house is tall and the shingles are gray because of the salt from the sea... Yes, I can keep a fire going at night. I do not know if I snore. Seal has never told me."

ANNA *(to CALEB, amazed)*. Did you really ask her about fires and snoring?

CALEB. I wished to know.

(JACOB enters from UR reading a letter.)

CALEB. Papa, what does your letter say? *(They move toward C.)*

JACOB. Sarah has said she will come for a month's time if we wish her to. *(Reading from the letter.)* "To see how it is. Just to see."

CALEB. I think...I think it would be good— *(Quickly.)* to say yes.

JACOB. Anna?

ANNA. Well. If it's only for a month. I—I guess so.

JACOB *(putting his arms around them)*. Well, then. I think we'd better get ready for some company. *(They exit UL chatting "She can have the good pillow," "I'll put flowers in her room," "We need to wash the curtains," "Do you think she'll bring her cat?" Etc.)*

SARAH *(standing and reading what she has written)*. "Dear Jacob, I will come by train. I will wear a yellow bonnet. I am plain and tall. Sarah. P.S. Tell them I sing."

CALEB'S VOICE *(from offstage)*. Hooray!

(SARAH exits as ADULT ANNA enters.)

ADULT ANNA. The day finally arrived when Sarah would come to our house. Papa got up early for the long day's trip to the train and back. He wore a clean blue shirt and a belt instead of suspenders. He fed and watered the horses as he hitched up the wagon.

JACOB'S VOICE *(from offstage DL)*. We've got a nice clear day, Bess.

ADULT ANNA. Old Bess. Calm and kind.

JACOB'S VOICE *(following an offstage "whinny")*. Settle down, Jack.

ADULT ANNA. Jack. Wild-eyed and ornery as ever. Papa leaned his head on Jack, and the horse settled down like he always did. And then Papa drove along the dirt road to fetch Sarah. Papa's new wife. Maybe. And maybe our new mother.

(ANNA enters from UL leafing through the bird book.)

ADULT ANNA. I still didn't know how I felt about her coming. She seemed nice enough in her letters. And she had sent me a lovely book. But a new mother? Something just didn't feel quite right. I was nervous about Sarah's visit. *(ANNA looks up from the book, lost in thought.)* But I knew *she* must have been nervous, too— coming halfway across the country to meet people she didn't even know. Even though I wasn't sure I wanted her to come, at least I could understand how she must have felt the day she left.

(She and ANNA exit UR and UL respectively as WIL- LIAM enters the parlor carrying a trunk.)

WILLIAM *(calling to offstage behind him)*. Sarah, the coach should be here any minute.

SARAH'S VOICE *(from offstage)*. I'm almost ready.

WILLIAM. Looks like good weather. Have you packed food for yourself? Five days is a long time on a train.

MEG'S VOICE *(from offstage)*. They serve food on a train, William.

WILLIAM. Ayuh. But it'll be expensive, I'll bet.

(MEG and SARAH, dressed for the trip and wearing a yellow bonnet, enter. SARAH carries a package and a handbag.)

MEG. Here we are. Doesn't she look lovely?

SARAH. I look—plain and tall.

WILLIAM. And nervous.

SARAH *(a slight smile)*. Yes. That, too. *(To MEG who helps straighten SARAH's shawl or dress.)* Thank you, Meg, for helping me.

MEG. What's a sister-in-law for?

SARAH *(a wry smile)*. Maybe to try and get somebody else married off as well?

MEG. Only if she wants to... And I mean that sincerely.

SARAH. I know you do.

(She squeezes MEG's hand or kisses her on the cheek. EBEN, a coachman, enters at DR and goes to the "front door" of the parlor.)

EBEN. Morning, everyone. Ready to go, Miss Wheaton?

SARAH *(taking a deep breath)*. Ayuh. I think so, Eben.

EBEN. Train leaves in two hours. Best to get there early.

SARAH. I know.

EBEN. I'll take the trunk, Mr. Wheaton.

WILLIAM *(as he hands the trunk to EBEN)*. Do you have everything, Sarah? Your ticket—money—gifts for the children?

SARAH. Yes, I'm sure I have everything. *(A pause, then almost in shock.)* Except for *Seal!*

MEG. Oh, my goodness. How could we forget Seal? We had her ready to go before we had *you* ready. I'll get her. *(She exits.)*

WILLIAM. Write to us as soon as you get there.

SARAH. I will.

WILLIAM. And come home if there's any reason at all not to stay. This house has plenty of room for all of us.

SARAH. Thank you, William.

(They embrace as MEG enters carrying a basket with a lid which has a cat's tail hanging out. SARAH takes the basket.)

SARAH. Oh—dear Seal. *(She peeps into the basket.)* I have a feeling she'll take the train ride better than me. *(A deep breath.)* Well ... Goodbye.

MEG *(very sincerely)*. Good luck to you, dear sister.

SARAH. Thank you, Meg.

WILLIAM. Take care. And *write*.

SARAH. Yes. I will.

WILLIAM *(as SARAH and EBEN leave)*. Thank you, Eben.

EBEN. My pleasure, Mr. Wheaton. I'll see that she gets to the station safe and sound.

(He and SARAH exit at DR as WILLIAM and MEG wave to them. A moment later, MEG begins to sniff and dab at her eyes with a handkerchief.)

WILLIAM. Meg, darling. What's wrong?

MEG. I—I think I miss her already.

WILLIAM. But—I thought you wanted her to go.

MEG. I do. But I don't. But—I guess I *do* more than I *don't*.

WILLIAM *(after a brief pause)*. Meg, if I ever figure you out—please don't let me know.

(They laugh and exit arm in arm. A moment later, CALEB enters from UL, goes to DL and looks toward offstage.)

CALEB. They're here! They're here!

(ANNA enters from UL.)

ANNA. Papa and Sarah? Already?

CALEB. No. The Nordstroms. Remember? They're coming to help get things ready.

ANNA. But we're already ready.

CALEB. Papa said they wanted to come and help.

ANNA. I think they just wanted to come and look at Sarah.

CALEB. I don't blame them. I can't wait to see her myself.

(ROSE and VIOLET enter running from DL.)

ROSE. Hello, Anna.

VIOLET. Hi, Caleb.

CALEB. Hello, Rose and Violet.

ANNA. Hello.

(MATTHEW and MAGGIE, carrying a covered basket, enter from DL.)

MATTHEW. Well, the big day has come.

MAGGIE. Are you excited?

CALEB. I am, you bet. But I don't think Anna is.

MAGGIE. Oh?

ANNA. I'm just nervous. That's all.

MAGGIE. I'm sure everything will be fine.

ROSE. Anna, you and Caleb look nice.

ANNA. Thank you.

CALEB. Is my face clean? Maybe it's too clean. Can a face be too clean?

VIOLET. Your face is clean, Caleb. But not too clean.

CALEB. I hope she's nice. Like Maggie.

MAGGIE. Why thank you, Caleb.

CALEB. How far away is Maine?

MATTHEW. Far away. By the sea.

CALEB. Will she like us? ... Of course she'll like us.

ROSE. Mama, can we play hide-and-go-seek?

MAGGIE. Not today, Rose. We have to help Caleb and Anna get ready for their guest. And then get on back home.

ANNA. You're not going to stay and meet Sarah?

MAGGIE. Not today, dear. That's for you and Caleb and your papa. We'll come back around in a few days when you've all gotten acquainted.

MATTHEW. Okay. Chores. Have they all been done? Chickens and hogs?

ANNA. I fed the chickens and gathered the—oh, no. I forgot to gather the eggs.

MATTHEW. Caleb?

CALEB. I fed the pigs some dried corn, and then I—I— Wait a minute. I forgot to slop the hogs. (MATTHEW and MAGGIE laugh.)

MAGGIE. I guess you can be excused for forgetting chores on a day like this.

MATTHEW. Caleb, you and I'll gather the eggs and feed the hogs. We'll let the ladies take care of the house. *(He and CALEB exit UR.)*

MAGGIE. Come on, girls. We'll dust a bit and make sure the beds are made. *(She and ROSE exit UL as VIOLET and ANNA follow behind. VIOLET stops ANNA before they exit.)*

VIOLET. Anna, you really do look nice. I wish Judson Moffet could see you.

ANNA *(making a face)*. Judson Moffet?

VIOLET. Yes. He likes you.

ANNA. No, he doesn't. And I can't stand him. He teases me at school.

VIOLET. But Mama says when boys tease girls it means they like them. And Jimmy Breyerson must really like me, 'cause he teases me something fierce.

ANNA. Well, Judson Moffet doesn't like me, and I don't like him, and that's a fact.

MAGGIE'S VOICE *(from offstage)*. Violet, Anna, come inside and make sure all the windows are open. The house needs freshening up a little.

ANNA. Okay, Maggie.

VIOLET. We're coming, Mama.

(ANNA and VIOLET exit UL. A moment later JACOB enters at DR and walks a few steps L, perhaps mopping his brow with a handkerchief. He paces a bit, appearing somewhat nervous. A train whistle is heard offstage R. LEVI, a stationmaster, enters from DR looking at his pocket watch.)

LEVI. Well, here she is, Jacob. Only twenty minutes behind schedule. Not bad for the Union Pacific.

JACOB. I was afraid I'd have to wait longer.

LEVI. Well, I'm glad you didn't. And you know why?

JACOB. Why?

LEVI. The way you've been pacing back and forth, I was
afraid you'd wear out the floor of the waiting area. *(They
chuckle.)* I remember when Matthew Nordstrom was
waiting for Maggie's train. I was afraid he was going to
pass out and fall right across the tracks. Now wouldn't
that have been a fine howdy-you-do? *(The train is heard
pulling in offstage.)* Well, I'll go meet the train and
show your guest to the waiting area.

JACOB. Thank you, Levi. *(LEVI exits DR as JACOB begins to "rehearse" his introduction.)* "Good afternoon,
Miss Wheaton"... No, that's a little stuffy... "Afternoon, Sarah Elisabeth"... That's better. Or maybe—
"Hello, Sarah"... Yes, that's it. "I'm very pleased"...
"I'm very *glad* that you"... *"We're* very glad that you
could come. Welcome to our fair state—and we hope
you enjoy your visit at our modest, but cozy farm."
There. That's it.

*(He continues rehearsing to himself. SARAH enters DR,
unseen by JACOB. She carries her purse, the box and
basket.)*

SARAH. Mr. Witting?

JACOB. Oh. *(He turns and sees SARAH.)* Uh—uh. Afternoon, uh, Miss Wheaton. We're very modest—to have
you enjoy our farm with your visit—and hope it's cozy.
(A brief pause.) No, no, no. That's not it. *(They laugh.)*

Let me try this again...Hello, Sarah. I'm glad you're here.

SARAH. So am I, Jacob. So am I. *(After an awkward moment, they shake hands.)*

JACOB. Here, let me help you with some of these things.

SARAH *(handing him the box)*. I—I hope I described myself accurately.

JACOB. Well, you *are* tall. But I wouldn't call you plain exactly. I think you're—

(LEVI enters from DR.)

LEVI. Jacob, I put Miss Wheaton's trunk in your wagon. It wasn't all that heavy.

JACOB. Thank you, Levi.

LEVI *(to SARAH)*. No offense, ma'am, but I hope I don't see you at this station again for a long, long time. Hope you understand.

SARAH *(smiling)*. I do. Thank you very much. *(LEVI tips his hat and exits DR.)*

JACOB. Well, on to the wagon. I brought my two finest horses today. Well...my *only* two horses. *(They laugh.)* Bess and Jack. But watch yourself around Jack. He can be a tough one.

SARAH. I can handle myself with animals.

JACOB *(seeing the tail protruding from the basket)*. Good. *And* I see you brought one along yourself.

SARAH. Seal. My cat.

JACOB. She'll be good in the barn. Help keep the mice away.

SARAH. She'll be good in the house, too.

JACOB. Well, better be getting on.

SARAH. Yes. I can't wait to meet the children.

(They exit at DR. A moment later, CALEB enters from UL, goes to C, puts his hand above his eyes and peers straight ahead into the distance.)

CALEB. Look, everybody! I can see dust way out there.

(MAGGIE, MATTHEW, ROSE, VIOLET, and ANNA enter from various areas.)

MAGGIE. Don't tell me they're coming back so soon.

MATTHEW. The Union Pacific is always late. Must have been on time for a change.

MAGGIE. Come on, girls. We need to get going.

ROSE. Do we have to?

VIOLET. We want to see Sarah.

MATTHEW. Another time. This is a special day just for the Witting family. Right, Anna?

ANNA. I guess. But it's been a lot of bother getting things ready.

CALEB. Look, they're getting closer.

MAGGIE. Let's go. Goodbye, Anna...Caleb.

CALEB *(hardly noticing them as he stares straight ahead)*. Goodbye.

ANNA. Thank you for helping us.

(MATTHEW, MAGGIE, ROSE and VIOLET exit DL, calling back "goodbyes.")

CALEB. I'm so excited.

ANNA. Settle down, Caleb. It may not be them anyway. It could be Mr. Titus. The man who wants to sell Papa a new cow.

CALEB. Wait. I think I can see the heads of the horses... Yes! Jack's making Old Bess run for her life!

ANNA *(staring out intently)*. You know—I think for once you may be right.

CALEB. Look. They're rounding the windmill and the barn. *(They look slightly R as though following the wagon with their eyes.)*

ANNA. Now they're coming along the Russian olive wind-break Mama planted. *(Their eyes go back to C then slightly L.)*

CALEB. A bonnet! I see a yellow bonnet! *(Dogs are heard barking offstage.)*

ANNA *(calling to the dogs)*. Hush, Nick! Be quiet, Lottie!

CALEB. They're here. *(They look offstage DL as horse whinnies are heard.)*

JACOB'S VOICE *(from offstage)*. Easy, Jack... Good girl, Bess.

CALEB. She *is* tall.

JACOB'S VOICE. This way, Sarah. I'm sure the children are waiting for us in the yard.

(CALEB takes two eager steps toward JACOB's VOICE. ANNA, a bit uncertain, moves back a step or two. JA-COB, carrying the trunk, and SARAH, holding her other belongings, enter from DL.)

JACOB. Hello, children... This is Sarah.

SARAH. Anna... Caleb.

CALEB. Did you bring some sea?

SARAH. Something *from* the sea. And me. And Seal, too.

CALEB *(looking inside the basket)*. Look, Anna, she *is* gray.

SARAH. Just like a seal.

JACOB. Well, why don't I take the cat and the trunk into your room, Sarah— *(He takes the basket from SARAH.)* —while you get acquainted with the children. *(He exits UL as SARAH opens the box.)*

SARAH. Caleb, hold out your hand. *(CALEB holds out his hand as SARAH gives him a shell from the box.)*

CALEB. A shell.

SARAH. It's called a moon snail. The sea gulls fly high and drop the shells on the rocks below. When the shell is broken, they eat what's inside.

CALEB. That's very smart.

SARAH *(handing ANNA a stone from the box)*. For you, Anna. A sea stone.

ANNA *(subdued)*. Thank you... It's smooth and white.

SARAH. The sea washes over and over the stone until it is round and perfect.

CALEB. That is smart, too... We do not have the sea here.

SARAH *(looking into the distance)*. No. But the land rolls a little—like the sea. *(For a moment there is a look of loneliness about her. She swallows hard as CALEB and ANNA glance at each other. SARAH recovers with a smile and reaches into the box again.)* Well, here are a few more shells. *(Distributing the shells to ANNA and CALEB.)* A scallop. A sea clam. An oyster. A razor clam. And the prettiest of all—a conch shell.

CALEB. Look at that!

SARAH *(putting the shell to her ear)*. If you put it to your ear, you can hear the sea.

CALEB. Let me try. *(SARAH gives him the shell which he puts to his ear.)*

SARAH. Well?

CALEB. I think I *can* hear it. It goes "shhhhh"— Here, Anna, you try it. *(He puts the shell to her ear.)*

ANNA. I—I don't think I hear anything.

SARAH *(aware of ANNA's distance)*. That's all right. Maybe you will—in time.

(JACOB enters from UL.)

JACOB. Your room is ready, Sarah. And Seal has already made herself at home. I see Maggie brought some corn muffins and apple butter. That should make a fine snack this afternoon.

SARAH. It sounds good to me.

JACOB. Well—let's go in. *(They start to leave.)*

CALEB. Papa, put this shell up to your ear. Sarah says you can hear the sea. And I did. But Anna didn't. *(He gives the shell to JACOB who puts it to his ear.)* Do you hear the sea, Papa?

JACOB. Well, I don't rightly know. I've never heard the sea before. But if you and Sarah heard it—I'll take your word for it.

(He, CALEB and SARAH laugh and exit UL, followed by ANNA. ADULT ANNA enters and watches them leave.)

ADULT ANNA. The dogs loved Sarah first. Lottie slept beside her bed, and Nick leaned his face on her covers in the morning. No one knew where Seal slept. She was a roamer... Papa was quiet and shy with Sarah. So was

I. I still didn't know how I felt about a stranger coming into our home and being our mother. But Caleb had no such thoughts. He talked to Sarah from early morning until the light left the sky.

(She exits as SARAH enters from UL carrying a large flower basket. CALEB enters right behind her.)

CALEB. Sarah, where are you going?

SARAH. Out to the field.

CALEB. To do what?

SARAH. To pick flowers.

CALEB. To put in the house?

SARAH. Some of them. The others I'll hang up so they'll dry out.

CALEB. Why do you dry them out?

SARAH. That way they'll keep some of their color, and we'll have flowers all winter long.

CALEB. All winter? Does that mean you'll stay?

SARAH. We'll see.

CALEB. Can I come and pick some flowers with you?

SARAH. Of course.

(ANNA, unseen by SARAH and CALEB, enters from UL. She stops and keeps her distance.)

CALEB. What kind of flowers will we pick?

SARAH. Prairie violets and bride's bonnet, I suppose. We don't have those where I live.

CALEB. What flowers *do* you have there?

SARAH. Oh, seaside goldenrod, wild asters, woolly rag-wort—

CALEB. Woolly ragwort! *(He takes SARAH's hand and pulls her toward offstage UR. He sings to his own tune.)*
> **WOOLLY RAGWORT ALL AROUND,**
> **WOOLLY RAGWORT ON THE GROUND.**
> **WOOLLY RAGWORT GROWS AND GROWS,**
> **WOOLLY RAGWORT IN YOUR NOSE.**

(He and SARAH exit UR laughing. JACOB, having entered DL just as they were leaving, also laughs. He carries two milk buckets as he goes to ANNA.)

JACOB. Caleb sure seems to like Sarah.

ANNA. I suppose.

JACOB *(a pause)*. What about you?

ANNA. What do you mean?

JACOB. What do *you* think of her?

ANNA. She's all right...I guess.

JACOB. Just—all right?

ANNA. So far.

JACOB *(putting his arm around her)*. Remember what we agreed on. All three of us have to want her to stay. And *she* has to want to stay, of course. Otherwise, she'll go back at the end of the month.

ANNA. I know.

JACOB. I have to go to the barn now and milk the cows. You might want to shell some corn for the chickens. We're getting a little low on feed.

ANNA. Okay, Papa. *(He starts to leave.)* Papa?

JACOB. Yes?

ANNA. Did you—did you say goodbye to Mama—before she—she—

JACOB. Yes... Why do you ask?

ANNA. I—just wondered.

(JACOB exits UR. ANNA exits slowly DL as ADULT ANNA enters.)

ADULT ANNA. Sarah had been with us for only a few days, but already I was pretty certain I didn't want her to stay. I knew my decision would hurt Caleb. And I felt bad about that. He was my brother—a sweet brother really. He *did* pester me a lot. But all brothers do that. No... I just couldn't accept Sarah. Actually, it was something else I couldn't accept. But at the time I wasn't quite sure what it was.

(She exits as CALEB, holding a bunch of flowers, and SARAH, carrying a basket of flowers, enter from UR.)

CALEB. Papa, Papa! Anna, Anna! Look what we picked. Flowers. Lots of flowers. Where are you, Papa?

(JACOB enters from UL.)

JACOB. Just putting the milk in the wellhouse. *(Looking at the flowers.)* Now that's quite a gathering.
CALEB. Sarah says we'll dry them, then we can look at them all winter long.
JACOB. Really?
SARAH. Ayuh.
CALEB. What does "ayuh" mean?
SARAH. In Maine it means yes.
CALEB. Oh, Papa—guess what else?
JACOB. What?

CALEB. Sarah taught me a song.

(ANNA enters from DL but stays in the background.)

JACOB. She did?

CALEB. Ayuh. *(They laugh.)*

SARAH. He refused to pick a single flower until I sang a song.

CALEB. And it's a special song, because it's about the month of May—when Sarah got our letters and we got hers. *(Somewhat melodramatically, as though telling a story.)* And then the next month, Sarah came to Kansas and stayed forever and ever. *(SARAH and JACOB exchange nervous laughter.)*

SARAH. Well, we'll see about that.

CALEB. Sing it, Sarah. Sing the song.

SARAH. Only if you'll sing it with me.

CALEB *(suddenly shy)*. I don't know if I remember the words.

SARAH. You certainly know the chorus. You were singing it all the way back from the fields.

CALEB. Well, okay. If Papa and Anna sing along with us.

ANNA. I'll just listen, thank you.

JACOB *(after a moment)*. In that case, I'll listen along with Anna. You two go ahead and sing.

CALEB. Okay. Sarah will sing the—the—what's the first part called again?

SARAH. The verse.

CALEB. That's right. Then I'll sing the chorus with Sarah. Can we do the whole song?

SARAH. Of course. We'll stop only if the horses start to stampede.

(She, CALEB and JACOB laugh. Note: During the song, JACOB bobs his head and/or taps his foot to the rhythm, whereas ANNA remains passive.)

SARAH *(singing)*.

    WE ROAMED THE FIELDS AND RIVERSIDES
    WHEN WE WERE YOUNG AND GAY;
    WE CHASED THE BEES AND PLUCKED THE
        FLOW'RS,
    IN THE MERRY, MERRY MONTH OF MAY.

SARAH & CALEB.

    OH, YES, WITH EVER-CHANGING SPORTS,
    WE WHILED THE HOURS AWAY;
    THE SKIES WERE BRIGHT, OUR HEARTS WERE
        LIGHT,
    IN THE MERRY, MERRY MONTH OF MAY.

SARAH.

    OUR VOICES ECHOED THROUGH THE GLEN
    WITH BLITHE AND JOYFUL RING;
    WE BUILT OUR HUTS OF MOSSY STONES,
    AND WE DABBLED IN THE HILLSIDE SPRING.

SARAH & CALEB.

    OH, YES, WITH EVER-CHANGING SPORTS,
    WE WHILED THE HOURS AWAY;
    THE SKIES WERE BRIGHT, OUR HEARTS WERE
        LIGHT,
    IN THE MERRY, MERRY MONTH OF MAY.

JACOB. That was pretty good singing. And I think you should be rewarded. Let's all go in and have some biscuits smothered in butter and molasses. That'll stick to our ribs for the rest of the day. *(They laugh and begin to exit as SARAH puts her arm around CALEB, and JACOB puts his arm around ANNA.)*

SARAH & CALEB *(singing as they leave).*

**OH, YES, WITH EVER-CHANGING SPORTS,
WE WHILED THE HOURS AWAY;
THE SKIES WERE BRIGHT, OUR HEARTS WERE
    LIGHT,
IN THE MERRY, MERRY MONTH OF MAY.**

(They exit UL as HOWIE, the postman, enters from DR.)

HOWIE *(calling out).* Morning, Wheatons. Mail for you today.

(WILLIAM enters the parlor and goes to the "front door.")

HOWIE. A catalog. And looks like a letter from Miss Sarah.

WILLIAM *(taking the mail).* Thank you, Howie.

HOWIE. Hope she's doing all right out there.

WILLIAM. So do we, Howie, so do we.

HOWIE *(looking skyward).* Looks like a storm a-brewin'.

WILLIAM. Yes. That's why I'm home today working on my nets.

HOWIE. When you write Miss Sarah, give her my best.

WILLIAM. I will, Howie. Thank you.

(HOWIE exits DR as WILLIAM quickly opens the letter and reads to himself. MEG enters behind WILLIAM, creeping up on him.)

WILLIAM. Good ... good ... good. *(MEG puts her hands over WILLIAM's eyes from behind.)* Bad. *(MEG takes her hands away. They laugh and give each other a quick kiss.)* A letter from Sarah.

MEG *(immediately interested)*. Oh. And how are things?

WILLIAM. Fine, so far. But this was written six days ago. Just after she arrived.

MEG. Well, if things were fine then, I'm sure they're even better now.

WILLIAM. We'll see what she says in her next letter.

MEG. Do you think she'll come back home for a little visit before she and Mr. Witting get married?

WILLIAM. Meg, darling. I wouldn't start planning the ceremony just yet. Things can change.

MEG. Oh, very well. I'll wait till we hear from Sarah again before I start baking the wedding cake. *(They laugh as they start to leave.)*

WILLIAM. That's my girl.

(They exit as SARAH and MAGGIE enter from UL carrying two bowls each, one filled with peas in pods, the other empty.)

MAGGIE. This was a good idea, Sarah. Shelling the peas outdoors instead of the kitchen.

SARAH. In Maine when we get a warm day like this we do almost everything outside. *(They sit and begin to shell the peas. They are quiet for a moment.)*

MAGGIE. You miss your home, yes?

SARAH. A little. Or maybe more than a little.

MAGGIE. I miss the hills of Tennessee sometimes.

SARAH. I miss the sea. And my brother. But he is married now. The house is hers. *(A soft laugh.)* I even miss my three old aunts who squawk like crows at dawn.

MAGGIE. There are always things to miss. No matter where you are.

(CALEB, ANNA, ROSE and VIOLET enter from UR, one after the other.)

CALEB *(bragging)*. I finished first. I finished all my chores first.

ANNA. That's because you're the youngest. And you don't have as many chores as us girls.

CALEB *(piously)*. I finished first because I'm the fastest. And I have the *most* chores to do.

ROSE. You do not, Caleb Witting.

VIOLET. We girls have the most to do.

CALEB. Do not.

ROSE. Do, too.

MAGGIE. That's enough, children.

SARAH. If you've finished your chores, you can help shell these peas. We're going to have a big pot full for supper. *(The CHILDREN sit and begin helping with the shelling.)*

VIOLET. What else are you having?

SARAH. Pork and greens. And hot cornbread.

ROSE. Mmm. Sounds good.

CALEB. Sarah, can Rose and Violet stay for supper?

SARAH. I don't see why not.

MAGGIE. Oh, but we have to get back and milk the cows, feed the chickens.

SARAH. Then we'll just eat earlier than usual. That way *you* won't have to cook anything tonight, Maggie.

MAGGIE. I think we'd better wait and see what the men have to say about it.

SARAH. If we're doing the cooking, I think it should be what the *women* have to say about it.

CALEB. Does that mean they can stay for supper?

SARAH. Of course. *(CALEB, ROSE and VIOLET shout, "Hooray," "Goody," etc.)*

MAGGIE. Well, in that case, we'd better shell the peas a little faster.

VIOLET. I wish we were shucking corn instead.

SARAH. Why, Violet?

VIOLET. Because if you shuck a *red* ear of corn, you get to kiss whoever you wish. And I would kiss...Caleb! *(She embraces CALEB who squirms away.)*

CALEB. No, no, no, no, no, no, no! *(ALL laugh.)*

MAGGIE *(to SARAH)*. We have corn-shucking parties in the summer.

ROSE. Last year Violet shucked a red ear and tried to kiss Jimmy Breyerson. But he wouldn't let her.

VIOLET. Tattletale. *(ALL laugh.)* I'll bet if Anna shucked a red ear she would try to kiss Judson Moffet.

ANNA. Judson Moffet. Ugh.

SARAH. I've never heard of that custom.

MAGGIE. Corn shuckings are very important social events in these parts. There's even a song about it.

CALEB. Will you teach it to us, Maggie?

MAGGIE. No, dear. I'm pretty much tone deaf. I can tell a story, but I can't teach a song.

CALEB. Sarah, will you teach us a song like you taught me and Papa and Anna?

ANNA. Papa and I didn't learn it.

CALEB. Well, you could have.

SARAH. It's all right, Caleb. She doesn't have to join in if she doesn't want to. But yes—I will teach you a song. *(The CHILDREN, except ANNA, cheer.)* This is one my Aunt Harriet taught me when I was just about your age. It's called "Billy Boy."

MAGGIE. Oh, I remember that one.

SARAH. Now, I'll start the song. But a lot of the lines repeat themselves. So when I point to you—you'll sing. Ready?

CALEB, ROSE & VIOLET. Yes. We're ready. Go ahead. Etc.

SARAH *(singing).*

> OH, WHERE HAVE YOU BEEN, BILLY BOY,
>   BILLY BOY,
> OH, WHERE HAVE YOU BEEN, CHARMING
>   BILLY?
> I HAVE BEEN TO SEE MY WIFE,
> SHE'S THE JOY OF MY LIFE,
> SHE'S A YOUNG THING AND CANNOT LEAVE
>   HER MOTHER.
>
> DID SHE BID YOU TO COME IN, BILLY BOY,
>   BILLY BOY,
> DID SHE BID YOU TO COME IN, CHARMING
>   BILLY?
> YES, SHE BADE ME TO COME IN,
> THERE'S A DIMPLE IN HER CHIN,

(Pointing to the CHILDREN.)

SARAH, CALEB, ROSE & VIOLET.
**SHE'S A YOUNG THING AND CANNOT LEAVE
HER MOTHER.**

SARAH.
**DID SHE SET FOR YOU A CHAIR, BILLY BOY,
BILLY BOY,**
(Pointing to the CHILDREN.)

CALEB, ROSE & VIOLET.
**DID SHE SET FOR YOU A CHAIR, CHARMING
BILLY?**

SARAH.
**YES, SHE SET FOR ME A CHAIR,
SHE HAS RINGLETS IN HER HAIR,**
(Pointing to the CHILDREN.)

CALEB, ROSE & VIOLET.
**SHE'S A YOUNG THING AND CANNOT LEAVE
HER MOTHER.**

SARAH.
**CAN SHE MAKE A CHERRY PIE, BILLY BOY,
BILLY BOY,**
(Pointing to the CHILDREN.)

CALEB, ROSE & VIOLET.
**CAN SHE MAKE A CHERRY PIE, CHARMING
BILLY?**

SARAH.
SHE CAN MAKE A CHERRY PIE,

QUICK'S A CAT CAN WINK HER EYE,
(Pointing to the CHILDREN.)

CALEB, ROSE & VIOLET.
SHE'S A YOUNG THING AND CANNOT LEAVE
HER MOTHER.

SARAH.
DID SHE TELL YOU OF HER AGE, BILLY BOY,
BILLY BOY,
(Pointing to the CHILDREN.)

CALEB, ROSE & VIOLET.
DID SHE TELL YOU OF HER AGE, CHARMING
BILLY?

SARAH.
SHE IS THIRTY YEARS AND FOUR,
THEN SHE ADDED FIFTEEN MORE,
(Pointing to the CHILDREN.)

CALEB, ROSE & VIOLET.
SHE'S A YOUNG THING AND CANNOT LEAVE
HER MOTHER.

SARAH *(speaking, quickly).* One more time! *(Pointing to the CHILDREN and herself.)*

SARAH, CALEB, ROSE & VIOLET *(singing slowly, perhaps going up at the end).*
SHE'S A YOUNG THING AND CANNOT LEAVE
HER MOTHER.

(Cheers and laughter follow the song.)

ROSE *(counting on her fingers)*. Thirty years and four, then she added fifteen more— She was forty-nine years old!

SARAH. Very good, Rose.

VIOLET. I'd think you could leave your mother by then.

(JACOB and MATTHEW enter from DL.)

JACOB. Hello! That was pretty good singing we heard coming up the hill.

CALEB *(running to JACOB)*. Papa, Papa, Sarah taught us a new song.

ROSE *(running to MATTHEW)*. Papa, Papa. We're staying for supper.

MATTHEW. But we have to get back and do *our* chores.

ROSE. But Mama and Sarah said we could eat an *early* supper.

MAGGIE. Well ... *I* didn't say that—exactly.

SARAH *(quickly)*. It was my idea.

ROSE *(to MATTHEW)*. Can we, Papa?

CALEB *(to JACOB)*. Please, Papa?

JACOB *(a bit awkwardly)*. Well—we usually eat supper at the same time every night. But—well— *(Bearing up with a forced smile.)* —we don't want to disappoint the children—if they've been promised—do we? *(The CHILDREN, except for ANNA, cheer as JACOB and SARAH look at each other.)*

MAGGIE *(sensing a bit of tension in the air)*. Children— Matthew. Help me take these peas into the kitchen.

VIOLET. There are only four bowls, Mama, and they aren't very—

MAGGIE. Into the kitchen—please. We'll finish shelling inside. *(To CALEB who lingers.)* You, too, Caleb. Come on. *(ALL except JACOB and SARAH exit. SARAH stands and slowly turns away from JACOB.)*

JACOB *(evenly, but not angry).* Sarah, I wish you would consult me on important matters like these.

SARAH. Important ... matters?

JACOB. Like moving supper up to the middle of the afternoon. That's when we'll have to eat so the Nordstroms can get home in time to do their work.

SARAH. Are—you upset that I changed the evening meal? Or are you upset that I didn't ask your *permission* to change the evening meal?

JACOB. I wouldn't call it upset, but ... Sarah, as I see it, you are a guest here. And you are welcome. But as a guest you should abide by the family rules.

SARAH. I didn't realize the time of supper was a family rule.

JACOB. It's not—exactly. But there are other things.

SARAH. Other things?

JACOB. You wanted me to teach you how to plow.

SARAH. But you didn't want to teach me because you think a woman's place is in—and around—the home.

JACOB. I don't think I'm alone in that view. But anyhow, I *did* teach you to plow, and now you won't do it.

SARAH. Because I can't plow in a long dress.

JACOB. Maggie can.

SARAH. But she could plow a lot better *and* faster wearing *overalls*. Just as I could.

JACOB. Maybe women wear overalls in Maine, but that's not how we do things in Kansas.

SARAH. Jacob, it's not a matter of how things are done in Maine or Kansas or anywhere else. It's a matter of what makes sense. I would never deliberately do anything to embarrass or hurt you or anyone else. But I do choose to do those things that make life a little easier and more efficient. And wearing overalls is better than wearing dresses for certain jobs on a farm. When someone says, "That's not the way we do things here," I don't accept it, if it makes good sense to do otherwise.

JACOB *(after a brief pause)*. Well … I think you've made your position quite clear on the matter. *(He looks skyward.)* The sun says it's about ten o'clock. But we'd better go in and have the noon meal now if we're going to eat supper in the middle of the day. *(He exits UL as SARAH smiles wistfully and shakes her head. She looks toward offstage UR.)*

SARAH. Oh, there's Seal toying with a mouse. *(Calling to SEAL.)* Let the little creature go, Seal! *(To herself.)* She likes it here. And I've come to like it as well. But I don't know if either of us should get too comfortable.

(ANNA enters from UL carrying an egg basket. She goes toward DL.)

SARAH. Oh, hello, Anna. Where are you going?

ANNA. I forgot to gather the eggs in the back henhouse. Papa scolded me.

SARAH. I'm sorry.

ANNA. He doesn't usually scold me.

SARAH. Would you like me to help? It might make the job go faster.

ANNA. No, thank you. I can do it myself.

SARAH. Very well. *(ANNA starts to leave.)* By the way, Seal seems to have taken to you.

ANNA. Yes. I think so.

SARAH. She's a funny cat. She doesn't like just anyone.

ANNA. I see.

SARAH. Anna, I like you, too. But you don't seem so sure about me.

ANNA. I have to go now.

SARAH. Have I done something wrong?

ANNA. No.

SARAH. Would you rather I—go away when the month is over?

ANNA. That's up to you.

SARAH. No, I think it's very much up to you—and Caleb—and your papa. I don't want to force you to like me, but I would like you to give me a chance.

ANNA *(uncomfortable, but saying it anyway)*. I—I don't want anyone taking the place of my mother.

SARAH. I don't *want* to replace your mother. No one could. But I would like to have the opportunity to take a place *next* to her—in your heart.

ANNA *(blurting it out)*. You're nothing like my mother. She was warm—and loving—and *pretty*. *(She turns away, fighting tears.)*

SARAH *(after a pause)*. I see.

(ADULT ANNA enters and watches.)

SARAH *(after a moment, forcing a smile and looking toward offstage).* Well, I'd better go get that poor little mouse away from Seal. *(Calling to offstage as ANNA and ADULT ANNA watch her.)* Seal! Let go of the mouse. It deserves a chance, too, you know. *(She exits. ANNA turns and exits DL, crying softly.)*

ADULT ANNA. Sarah tried not to show it, but I saw the hurt in her eyes as she turned and walked away. What I had said was unkind—and unfair—and I knew it... But I wanted *Sarah* to decide not to stay. I didn't want to be the one to say no when the time came... I still couldn't admit to myself why I didn't want Sarah to marry Papa or for her to become our mother. But I did know that I had been acting childish. And I wasn't very happy about it. I wasn't looking forward to the next two weeks. But nothing prepared me for how it would all end. *(She exits.)*

CURTAIN—END OF ACT ONE

ACT TWO

(A few days later. WILLIAM, looking at a letter, enters the parlor, followed by MEG.)

MEG. What could have happened?

WILLIAM. I told you—things can change.

MEG. What else does she say?

WILLIAM. Nothing more. Just what I read to you. *(Reading from the letter.)* ... "I feel quite certain I will be returning home by the end of the month. Or, perhaps, even before." *(Disappointed, MEG turns away. WILLIAM puts his arm around her.)* Meg, darling.

MEG. Oh, William. You know I adore Sarah, but it's been so wonderful having the whole house all to ourselves.

WILLIAM. I know.

MEG. And I also feel bad for Sarah, too. I'm sure she wanted things to work out.

WILLIAM. You know—maybe I could put a small addition onto the house—make a separate place for Sarah. She might like that as well.

MEG. No. We won't separate her. She will live with us as before. I just need to be a little less selfish about the whole thing. I'll write her tonight and tell her she'll be welcome when she returns.

WILLIAM. Meg Merchison. *That's* the woman I married.

MEG. And that's the woman I'll always be. *(They embrace.)*

56

WILLIAM. You know, when I finish drying out the nets, I'm taking you into town for a strawberry phosphate at Doc Webb's drugstore.

MEG. And I'll pretend I'm your girlfriend again.

WILLIAM. What are you talking about? You still *are* my girlfriend. Now you just happen to be my wife as well.

(They laugh and exit as ADULT ANNA enters.)

ADULT ANNA. The summer turned warmer, and the crop gathering began in full. The farm was a busy place at that time of year... Papa and Sarah didn't talk about their disagreement, but they hadn't forgotten about it either. They were polite to each other—but nothing more.

(ANNA enters from UL, lost in thought.)

ADULT ANNA. I knew Papa was bothered that I hadn't taken to Sarah. He probably thought it was her fault. But, of course, it wasn't. She was always kind and generous toward me. And she never let on that I had hurt her feelings. But I knew I had... *and* that I needed to do something about it.

(JACOB enters from UR.)

JACOB. Good morning, Anna.

ANNA *(subdued)*. Hello, Papa.

JACOB. Is anything wrong? You seem down in the dumps lately.

ANNA. Maybe. A little.

JACOB. What happened?

ANNA *(avoiding the truth)*. Well, uh—it's Judson Moffet. He pulled my hair at church on Sunday.

JACOB. But that was three days ago. Are you still upset about it?

ANNA. He—he pulled my hair real hard. It hurt.

JACOB. Well, I'll just speak to his papa about that.

ANNA *(quickly)*. No, it's okay. It didn't hurt *that* bad. I think he was just teasing.

JACOB. Then—this isn't about Judson Moffet, is it.

ANNA *(a brief pause)*. No.

JACOB. What is it then?

ANNA *(another brief pause)*. I think maybe *I* hurt somebody.

JACOB. Oh?

ANNA. Somebody's feelings anyway.

JACOB. I see. Do you plan to do anything about it?

ANNA. I—I don't know.

JACOB. It might make you feel better. And it'll probably make the other person feel better, too.

ANNA. I know.

JACOB. But it's up to you.

ANNA. I know.

JACOB. I'm taking Caleb into town this afternoon to see the doctor about his tonsils. Scrub out the milk pails while we're gone.

ANNA. Okay, Papa.

JACOB. And if you feel like it, why don't you fix supper tonight.

ANNA. But Sarah always cooks supper now.

JACOB. I told her to take the night off—that we've got another fine cook around here.

ANNA *(brightening)*. Thank you, Papa. *(They laugh as he exits DL.)*

ADULT ANNA. It's funny, you know. When something's bothering you it always helps to talk to somebody else about it. Even though I hadn't told Papa everything that was inside me, I felt better already... And I knew what I had to do.

(She exits as SARAH enters from UL.)

SARAH. Hello, Anna.

ANNA. Hello.

SARAH. I don't suppose you'd like to pick some wild daisies with me.

ANNA. No, thank you. *(SARAH starts to leave at UR.)* But I *would* like to say something to you.

SARAH. Of course. Go ahead.

ANNA. I—I just wanted to tell you... I'm sorry.

SARAH. Sorry? For what?

ANNA. Those things I said to you the other day. Especially the part about my mother being pretty.

SARAH. I'm sure she was.

ANNA. But the way I said it—it sounded like I was saying *you're* not pretty.

SARAH. Well... I'm not.

ANNA. I think you are. And I also think you're warm and loving. And I'm sorry I hurt your feelings.

SARAH *(visibly moved)*. Thank you... When you apologize to someone, it makes both people feel better.

ANNA. That's what Papa said.

SARAH *(with a faraway look in her eyes)*. I once hurt somebody's feelings. But I was too proud to say I was sorry.

ANNA. Was she a friend of yours at school?

SARAH. No. I was out of school by then. And it wasn't a girl. It was a boy.

ANNA. Did you like him?

SARAH. Yes. And if I *had* apologized, things might have been different today.

ANNA. That means we might never have known you.

SARAH. Would that have been so bad?

ANNA. Yes... Well, maybe. I—I don't know. I'm just not sure about things right now.

SARAH. That happens to me sometimes, too. And do you know what I do to clear my head?

ANNA. What?

SARAH. I take a nice, cool swim in the sea.

ANNA. But there's no sea here.

SARAH. There's a cow pond.

ANNA. We can't swim in the cow pond.

SARAH. Why not? There's a fresh spring running right through it, so it's perfectly safe to swim in.

ANNA. But—we don't have any swimming clothes.

SARAH. We have our slips and pantaloons.

ANNA. Our underwear?

SARAH. We're the only ones here. Your papa took Caleb to the doctor. They won't be back till supper.

ANNA. But—I don't know *how* to swim.

SARAH. I'll teach you. The cow pond is much easier to swim in than the sea.

ANNA *(getting excited)*. Well—I guess so, then.

SARAH *(taking ANNA's hand)*. Come on. We'll take off our dresses and leave them by the fence. *(She and ANNA exit at UR.)*

SARAH'S VOICE *(from offstage)*. This way our dresses won't get wet, and the cows won't step on them.

ANNA'S VOICE *(from offstage)*. I think this is going to be fun!

SARAH'S VOICE. Of course it will. And what's wrong with having a little fun now and then anyway?... Ready?

ANNA'S VOICE. Almost.

SARAH'S VOICE. Come on. Last one in is a rotten egg.

ANNA'S VOICE. Then I'll beat you— *(Her voice fades quickly in the distance.)* —'cause I don't want to be a rotten egg!

SARAH'S VOICE *(also fading in the distance)*. Hey, that's not fair! You got a head start! *(They are heard laughing in the far distance. A cowbell, followed by a mooing sound is heard offstage DL.)*

MR. TITUS' VOICE *(from offstage)*. Easy, Bossy. Easy girl.

(MR. TITUS, a farmer, enters from DL looking back over his shoulder.)

MR. TITUS. You stay tied to that tree now. I'm sure Mr. Witting is around here somewhere. *(He looks around.)* Mr. Witting!... Mr. Witting?... Well, what do you know about that. I come all the way out here to sell a man a cow, and he ain't home. I wish we'd hurry up and get them new inventions called telephones out this way. Sure would save a lot of aggravation. *(Calling off at UR.)* Mr. Witting!... Well, I'll just have to come back next week. *(He sees the offstage dresses.)* Now what's this? *(He exits UR.)*

MR. TITUS' VOICE. What in tarnation? ... Looks like two ladies dresses—a big lady and a little lady. *(He returns holding the dresses.)*

MR. TITUS. I'll bet these blew off the clothesline during that windstorm we had yesterday. I'll drape 'em across the branches of the tree Bossy's tied up to. *(The cowbell and mooing sounds are heard offstage.)* I'm coming, Bossy. Looks like you won't be a member of the Witting family for at least another week yet.

(He exits DL as ADULT ANNA enters.)

ADULT ANNA. Sarah and I had a wonderful time in the cow pond. First, she taught me how to float, then how to dog paddle. Nick and Lottie were nearby, and they came over to join us. They already knew how to dog paddle. Finally, Sarah taught me how to *really* swim—the first of many things she would teach me in the days to come.

ANNA'S VOICE. Oh, no!

SARAH'S VOICE. What's wrong?

ANNA'S VOICE. Our dresses are gone.

SARAH'S VOICE. Goodness. What could have happened to them?

ANNA'S VOICE. Maybe Nick and Lottie dragged them away.

ADULT ANNA. We didn't dare walk back to the house in our underwear, even though we didn't think anyone would see us. Finally, Sarah had an idea. We crept down to the barn and found what we needed.

(She exits as ANNA and SARAH enter from UR wrapped in colorful horse blankets. They giggle and laugh as they enter.)

SARAH. I don't think the horses will miss their blankets in this weather.

ANNA. This is the most fun I've had since Mama and I went berry picking. *(A pause as she reflects on it.)* We took sandwiches and lemonade and spent the whole day together—talking and laughing.

SARAH. I know you miss her—very much.

ANNA. It's not just that. I—I didn't tell her goodbye.

SARAH. But how could you? You were asleep when she—when she died.

ANNA. What I mean is, I didn't say good night to her ... on purpose.

SARAH. Oh?

ANNA. I—I was jealous of the new baby. And when Mama said he was so beautiful—I didn't think she loved me as much anymore. And I was paying her back by not saying good night. Papa said goodbye to Mama ... but I didn't.

SARAH *(a pause)*. Your mother is buried in the church cemetery, isn't she?

ANNA. Yes.

SARAH. Have you ever gone to her graveside alone?

ANNA. Not by myself. It's too far away. I'm always with Papa and Caleb—and sometimes our friends.

SARAH. What if you went to the cemetery all by yourself—and knelt down by the grave—and told your mother how you were feeling—and that you would like to say goodbye to her.

ANNA. But how would I get there?

SARAH. I can drive you in the wagon and drop you off at the cemetery. Then I'll go into town to pick up something I need. Something we both need actually. Then I can stop for you on the way back.

ANNA. But you don't know how to drive the wagon.

SARAH. I've watched your papa often enough. And I learn quickly.

ANNA. But Old Bess can't pull the wagon all by herself. And no one is allowed to take Jack out. He has a mind of his own.

SARAH. And so do I.

CALEB'S VOICE (*from offstage DL*). Sarah! Sarah!

JACOB'S VOICE (*from offstage DL*). Anna! Anna?

ANNA. We're out here, Papa!

(CALEB and JACOB, carrying the dresses, enter in a rush from DL.)

JACOB (*staring at ANNA and SARAH*). What in the world?

CALEB (*laughing*). Look at them.

ANNA. Where did you find our clothes?

JACOB. On the branches of the hickory tree—along with a note from Mr. Titus—the man who wants to sell me a cow.

SARAH. Oh, my. We had no idea he was here.

CALEB. We thought you had been eaten up by lions or tigers and all that was left were your clothes.

JACOB. Well, we didn't think *that* exactly. But we were a bit concerned.

SARAH. We're fine.

JACOB. What are you doing in those horse blankets?

ANNA. We couldn't find our clothes.

JACOB. I suppose you know what my next question is.

CALEB *(holding up his hand)*. I'll bet I know. "Why aren't you wearing any clothes?"

ANNA. We've been in the cow pond. Sarah taught me how to swim.

JACOB *(evenly)*. Why were you swimming in the cow pond?

SARAH. Because it's hot, and the pond is cool. What did the doctor say about Caleb?

JACOB. He's okay for now. We got some medicine in case his tonsils swell up again. The doctor was able to see Caleb earlier than we thought.

CALEB. Papa, I'm awful hot from the long ride home.

JACOB. It's a hot day. I'm hot, too. We all are.

CALEB. Not Anna and Sarah. They cooled off.

JACOB. In a very unusual way.

SARAH. Not unusual at all. People go swimming when it's hot.

CALEB. Papa, can I go in the cow pond?

JACOB. The cow pond is not a swimming hole. Anyway, there's nobody to watch you.

CALEB. Sarah could. She can swim. Anna, too—now.

SARAH. We have to go get dressed. *(She takes the dresses from JACOB.)* But that does leave one person who could watch you, Caleb. And maybe even go in the pond with you.

JACOB. Don't be ridiculous, Sarah. Anyway, we have nothing to swim in.

ANNA. Neither did we, Papa.

CALEB. Please, Papa.

JACOB. I've never even considered the idea of getting into a cow pond before.

SARAH. It's very refreshing.

JACOB *(seemingly flustered)*. Well of all the—I can't be-lieve what I'm— This is the silliest— I have only one thing to say about this ludicrous idea. *(He looks from one to the other, then glares at CALEB.)* Last one in is a rotten egg!

(He runs toward offstage UR as CALEB follows squeal-ing with delight as they exit. SARAH and ANNA laugh and shake hands, then exit UL as ADULT ANNA enters.)

ADULT ANNA. Three days later, Sarah and I were pre-sented with the opportunity to take the little trip we had talked about. Papa had gone to the back field to show Caleb how to plant potatoes. The field was already plowed, so they didn't need the horses. We knew that Papa wouldn't like what we were doing. But Sarah said the trip was too important to get into an argument with Papa over it. There would be plenty of time for an argu-ment *after* we got back.

(She exits as JACOB enters UL reading a note. He is obviously irritated. A moment later, a horse whinny is heard offstage.)

MATTHEW'S VOICE *(from offstage)*. Jacob! Where are you, Jacob?

JACOB *(calling to offstage)*. Is that you, Matthew?

(MATTHEW enters briskly from DL.)

MATTHEW. Jacob—are you and Caleb all right?

JACOB. You can see *I'm* okay. And Caleb's inside taking a nap.

MATTHEW. Well, that's a relief to know. Maggie thought she saw Sarah and Anna driving past our farm like a house afire. We were afraid something was wrong.

JACOB. Well, nobody's sick or anything. But I *would* say something's wrong. Sarah left this note saying she and Anna were going on an errand. She didn't ask. She just went. She's a headstrong woman, Matthew.

MATTHEW. Wouldn't you rather have a woman like that than one who always has to be told what to do?

JACOB. I think—I'd prefer one a little bit more in the middle. *(MATTHEW laughs.)* Maybe I'm behind the times when it comes to women, Matthew. But I don't see Maggie trying to be so—modern.

MATTHEW. Well, she's a little older than Sarah—maybe a bit more settled. But she does have her ways and opinions. And I'm glad she does.

JACOB. It's funny. Anna didn't seem to take to Sarah at first. But now she's starting to warm up to her. And I'm pleased about that. But now I'm starting to wonder how *I* feel about Sarah.

MATTHEW. You still like her, don't you?

JACOB. Well...yes. She's got some fine qualities. But there are a few things about her I'd like to change.

MATTHEW. Well, I wouldn't count on that if I were you.

JACOB. I guess not.

MATTHEW. But look on the bright side. You may not be able to change a woman. But the things you like about her won't change either. And that's a fact.

JACOB. You know, Matthew—you're a whole lot smarter than you look.

MATTHEW. I've been telling you that for years. *(They laugh.)* By the way, as I was pulling up, I noticed those three new lambs are getting pretty big.

JACOB. Oh, you mean Harriet, Mattie and Lou.

MATTHEW. Harriet, Mattie and Lou?

JACOB. Sarah named the lambs after her three aunts in Maine. She's given names to half the animals on this farm.

MATTHEW *(chuckling)*. That's quite an interesting woman you've got there, Jacob.

JACOB. Well, I don't have her yet. We still have to make our decision. And she has to make hers.

MATTHEW. That's true. Well—good day, Jacob.

JACOB. The same to you, Matthew. Thank you for your concern.

MATTHEW. What are next-door neighbors for? Even if they do live two miles away.

(They laugh as MATTHEW exits DL. JACOB begins to slowly pace back and forth. ADULT ANNA enters.)

ADULT ANNA. We knew Papa would be worried about us. And he was. But it was the kind of worry that turns to irritation when you find out the people you were worried about are okay. I decided that it was my obligation to step forward when Papa confronted us.

(She exits as two horses are heard whinnying offstage. JACOB puts the note in his pocket as SARAH and ANNA enter, each holding a wrapped bundle.)

JACOB. Sarah—Anna. I think I deserve an explanation for this.

SARAH. Yes, Jacob. You do. It was—

ANNA. —all my idea, Papa ... I—I wanted to visit Mama.

JACOB. Visit her?

ANNA. Where she's buried.

JACOB. But we visit her grave almost every time we go to church.

ANNA. I wanted to be with her all by myself this time.

JACOB. Sarah wasn't with you?

SARAH. I went into town to get some clothing for Anna and me.

JACOB. Anna has enough dresses.

SARAH. I didn't buy dresses.

JACOB. May I ask what you bought?

SARAH. We'll show you. *(She and ANNA remove the wrapping from the bundles and each holds up a pair of overalls.)*

JACOB *(trying to control his displeasure)*. Those are— pretty expensive overalls.

SARAH. I brought money from Maine. It's the same kind you use here in Kansas.

ANNA. Papa, they'll be much easier to work in. I won't have to watch the bottom of my dress when I feed the chickens. And I can climb up to the nests quicker when I gather the eggs.

JACOB *(to SARAH)*. So ... now you're dressing my daughter.

SARAH. The man at the store said he would take the overalls back if you don't approve. Anna won't wear them if you don't want her to.

JACOB. But you *will*?

SARAH. I am not your daughter. *(A horse whinny is heard offstage.)*

JACOB. I'm surprised Jack didn't rear up and turn the entire wagon upside down all over you.

SARAH. *Jack...* was a perfect gentleman.

JACOB *(evenly)*. I'm glad you're both all right. I'll go water the horses. *(He exits DL.)*

ANNA. Oh, Sarah. Maybe we shouldn't have gone. I'm afraid Papa might—might—

SARAH. —send me on my way next week when the month is over?

ANNA. Maybe.

SARAH. He has to know who I am, Anna—before either of us makes a decision. I like your papa very much. I think he's a good man. But he has to let me be the person I am. Nature has a unique way of making us who we are—and putting people together who belong together. *(A slight pause as she smiles.)* My mother once taught me a song about that. She used to sing it to William and me when we were children.

ANNA. Can I hear it?

SARAH. Maybe. But only if you'll sing it with me. I think you *are* overdue in that area. *(They chuckle.)*

ANNA. Yes, I guess I am.

SARAH *(singing)*.
> WHEN A TREE GROWS, IT GROWS.
> WHEN THE WIND BLOWS, IT BLOWS.
> THAT'S THE WAY THEY WERE MADE,
> LET THEM BE.
>
> WHEN A BIRD TWEETS A TUNE
> AND A WOLF HOWLS THE MOON,
> THAT'S THE WAY THEY WERE MADE,
> NATURALLY.

WE CANNOT CHANGE MOTHER NATURE'S
 WAY.
HER CAREFUL PLAN WE MUST OBEY.
NOR CAN WE CHANGE WHAT'S PLAIN TO SEE,
THAT YOU WERE MEANT FOR ME.
(Speaking.) Okay. Be ready when I point to you.
(Singing.)
 WHEN THE SEA ROARS—

*(Pointing to ANNA each time she is to sing, either solo
or with SARAH.)*

ANNA.
 —IT ROARS.

SARAH.
 WHEN THE RAIN POURS—

ANNA.
 —IT POURS.

SARAH.
 THAT'S THE WAY THEY WERE MADE,

ANNA.
 LET THEM BE.

SARAH.
 WHEN AN OWL WHISPERS, "WHO,"
 AND A COCK CROWS ON CUE,

ANNA.
 THAT'S THE WAY THEY WERE MADE,

SARAH.
NATURALLY.

(CALEB enters slowly from UL yawning, and sits—or stands—with SARAH and ANNA as they sing.)

SARAH & ANNA.
**WE CANNOT CHANGE MOTHER NATURE'S WAY,
HER CAREFUL PLAN WE MUST OBEY.
NOR CAN WE CHANGE WHAT'S PLAIN TO SEE,
THAT YOU WERE MEANT FOR ME.**

SARAH.
WHEN THE SUN SHINES—

(Pointing to ANNA and CALEB each time they are to sing together or with SARAH.)

ANNA & CALEB.
—IT SHINES.

SARAH.
WHEN THE VINE TWINES—

ANNA & CALEB.
—IT TWINES.

SARAH.
THAT'S THE WAY THEY WERE MADE,

ANNA & CALEB.
LET THEM BE.

SARAH.
> **WHEN A DOG WANTS TO GROWL,**
> **AND A CAT NEEDS TO PROWL,**

ANNA & CALEB.
> **THAT'S THE WAY THEY WERE MADE,**

SARAH.
> **NATURALLY.**

ALL.
> **WE CANNOT CHANGE MOTHER NATURE'S**
> **WAY,**
> **HER CAREFUL PLAN WE MUST OBEY.**
> **NOR CAN WE CHANGE WHAT'S PLAIN TO SEE,**
> **THAT YOU WERE MEANT FOR ME.**

(They applaud as SARAH embraces ANNA and CALEB. Near the end of the song, JACOB has entered from DL, unseen by the others, and looked on, pleased with what he has seen. He tries to creep away unnoticed, but he bumps into CHESTER UPSHAW, a salesman carrying a sample case who has entered from DL.)

CHESTER. Excuse me. I'm looking for the proprietor of this farm.

JACOB. That would be me. Jacob Witting.

CHESTER *(shaking hands with JACOB)*. Pleased to meet you, Mr. Witting. My name's Chester Upshaw. I represent the Silas A. Silverstone Shingle and Roofing Company of Topeka, Kansas. We're in the area surveying the damage perpetrated in these parts by the fierce tornado that tore through here last spring.

JACOB. We were pretty lucky, Mr. Upshaw. Didn't get a lot of damage.

CHESTER. But you did lose a few shingles, I perceive. Now the Silas A. Silverstone Shingle and Roofing Company is prepared to make you a fair offer on reshingling that roof, Mr. Witting. I just happen to have an array of samples right here—

JACOB. Thank you, Mr. Upshaw. But I doubt that I could afford the whole roof.

CHESTER. We have a generous payment plan.

JACOB. Well, I like to pay for things when I get them. Don't like to owe anybody anything.

CHESTER. I understand, Mr. Witting. Thank you for your time. But you should get those missing shingles replaced eventually. It's at least a two-man job. Here's my card if you should change your mind. *(He hands a card to JACOB.)* Thank you. And good day to you.

JACOB *(looking toward offstage)*. Say, is that an automobile you drove up in?

CHESTER. Brand new Model T. Company car of the Silas A. Silverstone Shingle and Roofing Company.

JACOB. Haven't seen one of those up close before. Mind if I take a look?

CHESTER. Not at all. Bring Mrs. Witting and the children, too. *(He exits DL as the OTHERS follow.)*

CALEB *(in a loud whisper to SARAH)*. He called you *Mrs. Witting.*

SARAH *(glancing at JACOB who smiles)*. It was a natural mistake, dear, a natural mistake.

(They exit DL as ADULT ANNA enters.)

ADULT ANNA. The month was almost over. Soon it would be time for a decision—from us *and* from Sarah. In my mind and in my heart, I now knew I wanted her to stay. But I didn't dare ask if she would. And I still wasn't sure how Papa felt about things... He had invited the Nordstroms to come over for a picnic on Saturday afternoon—just two days before Sarah would go—or stay. Everybody was a little nervous. But we weren't the only ones.

(She exits as WILLIAM, holding a letter, and MEG, enter the parlor.)

MEG. What does she say this time?

WILLIAM *(looking at the letter)*. Well...I'd call it neutral.

MEG. Neutral?

WILLIAM. Ayuh. Things are better with Anna, but not as good with Jacob.

MEG. When was it written?

WILLIAM. Five days ago.

MEG. Goodness. What could have happened in those five days?

WILLIAM. We'll just have to wait and see. But we'll know soon. If she's getting married, we'll get a letter. If she's not, we'll get Sarah herself.

MEG. Oh, I do hope it's a letter—for her sake as well as ours. I'm prepared for anything, but I *am* very nervous.

WILLIAM. Well, I guess we're both a little undone over the outcome. But do you know what settles nerves better than anything I can think of?

MEG. What?

WILLIAM. A walk into town and a strawberry phosphate at Doc Webb's drugstore.

MEG. Let's *run* into town and have a *double* strawberry phosphate at Doc Webb's drugstore.

WILLIAM. That's an even better idea than mine. Let's go.

(They laugh and exit quickly. A moment later, ANNA, CALEB, SARAH and the NORDSTROMS enter from UL, gathering for a picnic. They bring on various dishes and set them onto the table.)

SARAH. Okay, everybody. Spread everything out on the table there.

CALEB *(carrying on two rustic stools).* I brought these stools from the kitchen.

SARAH. Good boy, Caleb.

CALEB. Where's Papa?

SARAH. He's gathering some ears of corn. It's the first crop of the summer.

ANNA. That's why the big pot of boiling water is on the stove.

CALEB *(calling to offstage).* We're about ready to eat, Papa!

JACOB'S VOICE *(from offstage).* I'm on my way!

MAGGIE *(calling to offstage).* Jacob, I brought your favorite—peach marmalade!

(JACOB enters from UR carrying a bucket of unshucked corn ears.)

JACOB. Bless you, Maggie.

MATTHEW. *And* a big loaf of sourdough bread. Made it myself.

JACOB. You, Matthew?

MATTHEW *(his arm around MAGGIE)*. This woman I married has taught me a lot of things. Most of 'em I've forgotten, but not how to bake bread. *(ALL laugh.)*

MAGGIE. And I'll bet Sarah has taught the Wittings a few things as well.

CALEB. She taught me how to make lemonade with honey in it.

ANNA. She taught me how to swim.

CALEB. She taught us new songs.

ANNA. She taught us—

ROSE. Sarah, will you teach us a new song?

VIOLET. Please.

MAGGIE. They were hoping you'd sing something.

SARAH *(looking skyward)*. Maybe after we eat. It looks like some dark clouds are heading this way. We may be in for a storm.

CALEB. What color is the sea when it storms?

SARAH. Blue ... and gray and green.

JACOB. I think the weather will hold off a while longer, so I'll tell you what. Let's give Sarah a little break, and *I'll* teach you a song myself. *(The CHILDREN are delighted.)*

ANNA. You, Papa?

CALEB. You're going to sing?

JACOB. And why not? I used to sing a lot. And this song is perfect for the occasion. It's called "Shuckin' of the Corn"—which is exactly what we're about to do. *(The CHILDREN cheer. JACOB sings.)*

    I HAVE A SHIP ON THE OCEAN,
    ALL LINED WITH SILVER AND GOLD.
    BEFORE I'D SEE MY TRUE LOVE SUFFER,
    THAT SHIP WOULD BE ANCHORED AND SOLD.

> I'M A-GOIN' TO THE SHUCKIN' OF THE CORN,
> I'M A-GOIN' TO THE SHUCKIN' OF THE CORN,
> A SHUCKIN' OF THE CORN AND A BLOWIN' OF
>   THE HORN,
> I'M A-GOIN' TO THE SHUCKIN' OF THE CORN.

MATTHEW *(speaking)*. I know that song.

JACOB & MATTHEW *(singing)*.

> THE WIND BLOWS COLD IN CAIRO,
> THE SUN REFUSES TO SHINE.
> BEFORE I'D SEE MY TRUE LOVE SUFFER,
> I'D WORK ALL THE SUMMER TIME.

MATTHEW *(speaking)*. Come on. Everybody sing.

ALL.

> I'M A-GOIN TO THE SHUCKIN' OF THE CORN,
> I'M A-GOIN TO THE SHUCKIN' OF THE CORN,
> A SHUCKIN' OF THE CORN AND A BLOWIN' OF
>   THE HORN,
> I'M A-GOIN' TO THE SHUCKIN' OF THE CORN.

(Repeating the last two lines, going up at the end.)

> A SHUCKIN' OF THE CORN AND A BLOWIN' OF
>   THE HORN,
> I'M A-GOIN' TO THE SHUCKIN' OF THE CORN.

(ALL cheer.)

JACOB *(to MATTHEW)*. Matthew. I didn't know you
could sing.

MATTHEW *(sheepishly)*. Well, uh—

JACOB. And I still don't. *(ALL laugh as MATTHEW feigns pouting. He and JACOB then shake hands.)* Well, as tradition has it, the farmer who plants the corn gets to shuck the first ear from the harvest. Then everybody else shucks theirs, and we'll throw them into the boiling water. *(Looking into the bucket.)* Now...this looks like a nice plump ear. Let's see what it looks like. *(He shucks the corn, revealing a bright red ear. The CHILDREN react.)*

CALEB. Papa! You shucked a red ear of corn!

JACOB. Hmm. So I did. A red ear's kinda rare.

ANNA. You know what that means, don't you, Papa?

JACOB *(pretending not to know)*. Means it's red, I guess.

CALEB. No, Papa. If you shuck a red ear of corn, you get to kiss anybody you wish.

JACOB. You know...I think I've heard that before.

ROSE. Who are you going to kiss?

VIOLET. I'll bet it'll be Anna or Caleb.

JACOB. Oh, I don't know. I kiss them all the time as it is.

ANNA. How about Rose or Violet?

JACOB. Nah. They probably gets lots of kisses from Matthew and Maggie.

VIOLET. Yes, we do.

ROSE. Papa's beard tickles when *he* kisses.

JACOB. Then I'm sure not going to kiss him. *(The CHILDREN laugh.)* And I don't think Matthew would like it if I kissed Maggie. So—

ANNA *(to the other CHILDREN)*. That means there's only one person left.

VIOLET *(whispering)*. Sarah.

(JACOB crosses to SARAH.)

ROSE. If he kisses her, does that mean they have to get married?

CALEB. I hope so.

(JACOB takes SARAH's hand and she stands.)

SARAH *(a bit awkwardly)*. Jacob, those dark clouds seem to be getting closer. Maybe we'd all better go back inside now.

JACOB. Don't worry. I'm not going to do anything foolish. But I *am* going to hold onto this red ear of corn for possible future use. *(ALL laugh.)* No, I just wanted to tell Sarah what she has taught *me*. She's taught me patience, that's for sure. *(He and SARAH chuckle quietly.)* Understanding. Cooperation. Not to be quite so narrow-minded. But maybe the most important thing of all—she taught me I could sing again. *(To SARAH.)* Thank you. *(They gaze into each other's eyes for a moment until a large clap of thunder, followed by strong wind, is heard.)*

MATTHEW. Jacob, I do believe the heavens are applauding your little speech. *(The stage begins to darken as more thunder, followed by strong wind, is heard.)*

MAGGIE. *I* believe the heavens are telling us we're going to finish this picnic inside. Let's go!

(ALL begin to quickly gather up food, stools, etc. The thunder and wind continue amid the lines: "Hurry up, the rain's coming." "Don't leave anything outside." "Don't forget the corn, Jacob." "Are the horses in the barn?" "Children, help me with the food." Etc. As they exit UL, a full rainstorm is heard as the lights go almost

to black. After a few moments, the storm subsides as the lights come up, and ADULT ANNA enters.)

ADULT ANNA. We had our picnic indoors while the storm roared outside. It didn't last very long, but it uprooted a couple of saplings Papa had planted. And it blew a few more shingles off the roof. Matthew said he'd try to get over the first of the week and help put the shingles back on. *(A pause.)* When the storm was over, the Nordstroms left. And near nightfall Papa and Sarah took a walk in the fields.

(JACOB and SARAH enter from UL.)

SARAH. Jacob, are you sure you want to go for a walk? It's still awfully wet from the storm.

JACOB. The dampness will cool us off. Anyway, I thought it would be better if we were all alone—away from the children. I—I have something on my mind that I need to ask you.

SARAH *(with anticipation)*. Oh?

JACOB. *And— (Taking the red ear of corn from his pocket.)* —I also wish to uphold the tradition of the red ear of corn. *(They chuckle as he takes her hand and they exit UR.)*

ADULT ANNA. Caleb and I prayed all that night—and at church the next day—that Sarah would stay and marry Papa... Monday was the last day of the month. I was restless the night before. So was Caleb. We finally did get to sleep, but we didn't wake up until the sun was high in the sky Monday morning.

(She exits as JACOB enters from DL, seemingly upset. He calls to offstage.)

JACOB. Anna! Caleb! Are you up yet? I need to see you! Anna! Caleb!

(He paces a bit until ANNA and CALEB enter from UL, yawning.)

ANNA. What's wrong, Papa?

JACOB. Have you seen Sarah this morning?

CALEB. No, Papa, we just got up.

JACOB. Gracious. Sleeping like city folks.

ANNA. Maybe she went to pick flowers in the field.

JACOB. Well, if she did, that means somebody stole the horses and wagon. They're gone. See if she might still be asleep, Anna.

ANNA. Okay, Papa. *(She exits UL.)*

CALEB. Are you worried, Papa?

JACOB *(obviously very concerned)*. A little—maybe.

CALEB. Did you ask her to marry you, Papa?

JACOB. Yes...I *did* ask her...Saturday night.

CALEB. What did she say?

JACOB. She said she still had two more days to think about it, but she seemed glad that I asked her.

(ANNA enters from UL disheartened.)

ANNA. Papa?

JACOB. Yes?

ANNA. Sarah's gone...   And her trunk is gone, too.

CALEB. Oh, no.

ANNA. Do you think she went to the train station—without saying goodbye?

JACOB. It would seem so. Was there a note—or anything?

ANNA. No. She didn't even make up her bed. She always makes up her bed.

JACOB *(a pause)*. Well, you two start your chores. The pigs and chickens must be half-starved by now. The idea of sleeping this late on a work day.

CALEB. Papa, we stayed up hoping—and praying—

JACOB *(putting his arms around them)*. I understand. I didn't sleep very well myself last night. In fact, *I* got up later than usual. That's why I didn't see Sarah when she left... Well, you get on with your chores, and I'll take a walk to the Nordstrom farm. Maybe Matthew can drive me to the station to pick up the horses and wagon.

ANNA. Okay, Papa.

CALEB. 'Bye, Papa. *(Two horse whinnies are heard off-stage DL.)*

JACOB. That may be Matthew right now. He said he'd help with the shingles this week, but I didn't think he'd come so soon. I don't even have the replacement shingles yet. *(Calling to offstage.)* Hello, Matthew! Is that you?

SARAH'S VOICE *(from offstage)*. No. It's me.

ANNA. Sarah!

CALEB. She's back!

(SARAH enters from DL. She holds a small package.)

SARAH. Good morning, everybody. I'm sorry I didn't leave you a note. I was halfway to town before I realized I hadn't.

JACOB. Did you—forget something?

SARAH. Forget something?

JACOB. Weren't you going back to Maine? You took your trunk—your clothes.

SARAH. My trunk, yes. But my clothes are still in the chest of drawers.

ANNA. I didn't even look there.

SARAH. I wasn't going to Maine. I was only going to town. *(JACOB, ANNA and CALEB breathe sighs of relief.)* When I woke up, I saw the kind of clouds we had on Saturday. So I thought somebody should go and get some shingles for the roof. You were all fast asleep. Just like city folks. *(JACOB, ANNA and CALEB smile.)* So, I decided to go myself.

JACOB. Why did you take your trunk?

SARAH. To pack the shingles in so they wouldn't slide around and break.

CALEB. That's pretty smart.

SARAH. And I also got something for the children. *(Opening the wrapped package.)* Drawing paper and colored pencils. Blue, gray and green. Now I can show you what the sea looks like where I used to live.

ANNA. You said—"used to live." Does that mean you'll stay?

SARAH. If I'm still invited.

CALEB. And you'll marry Papa?

SARAH. If he still wants me.

ANNA. And you'll be our mother?

SARAH. I can't very well be married to your papa and *not* be your mother.

CALEB. What do you say, Papa?

JACOB. I have only one word. *(A brief pause, then loudly.)* A-yuh! *(ALL laugh and embrace.)* Children, get to your chores. Sarah, we can unload the shingles, and when Matthew comes, he and I—

SARAH. We don't need Matthew. I've replaced many a shingle on our roof in Maine.

JACOB. Then we'll get right to it.

SARAH. No. You have plenty of other duties to attend to. I'll put up the shingles myself.

JACOB. But the fellow from the roofing company said it's at least a two-man job.

SARAH. Maybe. But it's only a one-*woman* job if it's *this* woman. I'm a good carpenter. I work fast. And I'm not afraid of heights.

JACOB. Sarah Elisabeth Wheaton, you beat all. You're as tough and independent as your gray cat, Seal. And you know—I wouldn't have it any other way. *(Taking SARAH's hand.)* Let's go unload the trunk. *(They exit DL as ANNA and CALEB dance in a circle.)*

ANNA & CALEB. She's staying! She's staying! She's staying! *(They stop and look offstage where JACOB and SARAH exited.)*

ANNA *(in a loud whisper)*. Look. He's going to kiss her.

CALEB. And he doesn't even have a red ear of corn.

ANNA. Now she's kissing *him*.

CALEB *(a pause)*. Now they're looking at *us*.

JACOB'S VOICE *(from offstage)*. Children! Chores!

CALEB. Yes, Papa!

ANNA. Right away, Papa!

(They exit running UL as MEG enters the parlor, pacing nervously. She looks out the "front door," then paces again. WILLIAM enters from DR into the parlor.)

MEG. William!

WILLIAM. She wasn't at the train station.

MEG. And the mail hasn't come yet. When will we know?

WILLIAM. Actually, I *have* the mail. I met Howie on his route and saved him the trip.

MEG. Did we get anything—important?

WILLIAM *(taking out a few pieces of mail from his jacket pocket and flipping through them).* An invoice for the paint I used on the boat. An invitation to the church picnic. And...hmm. What's this? A letter from Kansas.

MEG. William! Did you open it yet?

WILLIAM. Of course. It was addressed to me.

MEG. What does it say?

WILLIAM *(handing the letter to her).* Read it yourself.

MEG *(reading to herself for a moment, then aloud).* "...And on August twenty-seventh of this year, I will become the wife of Mr. Jacob L. Witting." *(She starts to cry.)* Oh, William. *(He embraces her.)*

WILLIAM. Are you crying because you're happy—or sad?

MEG. A little of both. I'll miss Sarah, but I'm so happy for her.

WILLIAM. And now we have the house all to ourselves.

MEG. But I never realized how much room we had. *(They start to exit.)* You know, I hear there's a new school teacher coming to town in the fall. A single woman who might be looking for a place to live. I think Sarah's room might be the perfect place for a young—

(Her voice trails off and they exit as the lights fade to dim with only the pool of light on at DRC as at the beginning. ADULT ANNA enters wearing the hat but now with two more ribbons hanging down the back and roses on the brim. She mimes looking into the mirror.)

ADULT ANNA *(calling to offstage)*. It's perfect, Sarah. The ribbons in the back are just right, and I love the roses.

SARAH'S VOICE *(from offstage)*. Good. Now it's time to— Oh, just a minute, dear, there's someone at the back door... Well, look who's here. Anna—it's your fiancé.

ADULT ANNA. Tell him to come in, please.

SARAH'S VOICE. Very well. But he can't stay long.

ADULT ANNA. I know. *(To the audience.)* Oh, I think I forgot to mention—day after tomorrow is my wedding day. And I'll bet you can guess who I'm marrying. Mr. Judson Jeremiah Moffet... That's right—Judson.

(JUDSON enters into the pool of light.)

JUDSON. Hi, sweetheart! *(He swings her around as she protests good-naturedly.)*

ADULT ANNA. Judson, Sarah and I are very busy getting ready for the wedding.

JUDSON. I know. *(Teasing her.)* But I just thought I'd come by and make sure you didn't want to change your mind.

ADULT ANNA. If I did, Papa would kill me.

JUDSON. Oh, he likes me that much, does he?

ADULT ANNA. No. He's spending so much money on this wedding, I can't back out now. *(They laugh, and she embraces him.)* Nothing on earth could make me change my mind about you, Judson Moffet.

JUDSON. Well, not only are you the prettiest girl around, you're also the smartest. *(They kiss lightly.)*

SARAH'S VOICE. All right, you two! Anna and I have a wedding to get ready for.

JUDSON *(calling to offstage)*. I'm leaving right away, Sarah. *(To ANNA.)* I'm sure glad us fellows don't have to go through what you girls go through when *we* get married.

ADULT ANNA. Me, too. You'd look awful funny in a wedding dress. *(They laugh.)*

JUDSON. See you Saturday, sweetheart.

ADULT ANNA. And a lifetime of Saturdays after that. *(They kiss again, then JUDSON starts to leave.)* Oh, Judson. There's one more thing we need to do before the wedding.

JUDSON. What's that? *(She playfully pulls his hair, and he emits an exaggerated howl.)*

ADULT ANNA. I've owed you that for a long time. Now we can start our new life together on equal footing. *(They laugh and embrace. He blows her a kiss and exits.)* It seems like only yesterday that Papa and Sarah were getting married. I was so excited—wearing my best dress.

(The general lighting begins to come up. ANNA enters carrying a small bouquet of dried flowers.)

Caleb, looking handsome and happy.

(CALEB enters.)

Matthew and Maggie, Rose and Violet—wearing their Sunday best—on a Saturday.

(The NORDSTROMS enter.)

And even though Sarah's brother, William, and sister-in-law, Meg, couldn't make the long trip, they promised to sit in their own church in Maine during the exact hour of the wedding.

(WILLIAM and MEG enter.)

It was a splendid day. Not a cloud in the sky. And when it was over, Papa had a new wife, and Caleb and I had a new mother. Oh, and I caught the wedding bouquet. *(ANNA holds the bouquet in front of her and looks at it.)* Sarah dried it and preserved it, and it will be the very bouquet that I will carry on *my* wedding day. *(ANNA goes to ADULT ANNA, gives her the bouquet, then returns to her original place. If desired, the cast members on stage, except ADULT ANNA, begin to hum the verse to the song "Nature's Song.")* Many of the same people who were at *that* wedding will be at mine. And there will be new people, of course—including the Wheatons who'll be coming all the way from Maine. But none will be more important that day than the three people who will be at my side. Dear Judson...

(JUDSON enters.)

Darling Papa...

(JACOB enters.)

And my best friend in all the world... Sarah, plain and tall.

(SARAH enters. If desired, ALL sing the chorus of "Nature's Song.")

ALL.
> WE CANNOT CHANGE MOTHER NATURE'S
>   WAY,
> HER CAREFUL PLAN WE MUST OBEY.
> NOR CAN WE CHANGE WHAT'S PLAIN TO SEE,
> THAT YOU WERE MEANT FOR ME.

CURTAIN—THE END

PRODUCTION NOTES

CASTING

Minor Characters

The actor playing Judson Moffet may also perform the other minor roles. Or those roles may be assigned to 1-6 additional actors. While most, if not all, of the minor characters would likely have been male in the early 1900s, gender-blind casting is appropriate when necessary, hence the listing of alternate female names on the cast of characters page.

Cutting the Cast Size to Ten

While a cast of 12 is considered to be the optimal minimum, it is possible to bring the cast size down to 10 with doubling. In that case one actor would play the 7 minor characters while another actor would play both Matthew and William. One actress would portray both Maggie and Meg, thus making a cast of 4m and 6w.

In order to allow time for adequate costume changes for the actors who are doubling, four minor script modifications are necessary. The scenes and suggested alterations are as follows:

(1) Matthew and Maggie's entrance immediately prior to Sarah's arrival at the farm. The four children, who are on stage, may improvise a brief game of tag or hide-and-go-seek until Matthew and Maggie enter.

(2) Sarah and Maggie's entrance to shell peas. The four children enter before Sarah and Maggie. They carry chore items such as buckets, egg baskets, small gardening tools, etc., and argue about who has the hardest chore. They then exit UR as Sarah and Maggie enter.

(3) The entrance of Anna, Caleb, Sarah and the Nordstroms to prepare for the picnic. Matthew and Maggie do not enter with the others. The children will make two or three trips between the yard and the house with picnic items as directed by Sarah. Matthew and Maggie enter, when ready, on their first lines of the scene.

(4) Adult Anna's speech at the end of the play. Adult Anna will omit the line, "And even though Sarah's brother, William, and sister-in-law, Meg, couldn't make the long trip, they promised to sit in their own church in Maine during the exact hour of the wedding." William and Meg will not appear in the final wedding tableau.

MUSIC

The four songs in the play will most likely be sung a cappella; however, it would be appropriate, if desired, for Sarah to carry a pitch pipe. If the actress portraying Sarah can play a guitar, that instrument may be added to the luggage she carries to Kansas and used to accompany the three songs she sings. Three of the four songs in the play are in public domain. The fourth, "Nature's Song," written by the playwright, is under copyright and may be performed only in conjunction with the play. Rights for other uses of the song require express permission of Dramatic Publishing.

STAGING OF ADULT ANNA'S ENTRANCES

There are no specific directions in the script regarding the locales of Adult Anna's entrances and exits. They should vary among the four designated entrance areas in the interest of stage balance. At times, she may enter and exit from the same locale—at others, she may enter at one locale and exit at another.

Nature's Song

By Joseph Robinette

When the sea roars, it roars.
When the rain pours, it pours.
That's the way they were made,
Let them be.

When an owl whispers "who,"
And a cock crows on cue,
That's the way they were made
Naturally.

(repeat chorus)

When the sun shines, it shines.
When the vine twines, it twines.
That's the way they were made,
Let them be.

When a dog wants to growl,
And a cat needs to prowl,
That's the way they were made
Naturally.

(repeat chorus)

The Merry Merry Month of May

By Stephen Foster

We roamed the fields and riv-er sides, When we were young and gay; We chased the bees and plucked the flow'rs, in the mer-ry mer-ry month of May. Oh, yes, with ev-er chang-ing sports, we whiled the hours a-way; The skies were bright, our hearts were light-, in the mer-ry, mer-ry month of May

Our voices echoed through the glen
With blythe and joyful ring;
We built our huts of mossy stones,
And we dabbled in the hillside spring.

(Repeat chorus)

Billy Boy

Words and music traditional

Oh, - - - where have you been, Bil - ly Boy, Bil - ly Boy, Oh, -

where have you been, charm - ing Bil - ly? I have

been to seek a wife, She's the joy - of my life, She's a

young thing and can - not leave her moth - er.

Did she bid you to come in, Billy Boy, Billy Boy?
Did she bid you to come in, charming Billy?

Yes, she bade me to come in, there's a dimple on her chin,
She's a young thing and cannot leave her mother.

Did she set for you a chair, Billy Boy, Billy Boy?
Did she set for you a chair, charming Billy?

Yes she set for me a chair, she has ringlets in her hair,
She's a young thing and cannot leave her mother.

Can she make a cherry pie, Billy Boy, Billy Boy?
Can she make a cherry pie, charming Billy?

She can make a cherry pie, quick's a cat can wink her eye,
She's a young thing and cannot leave her mother.

Did she tell you of her age, Billy Boy, Billy Boy?
Did she tell you of her age, charming Billy?

She is thirty years and four, then she added fifteen more,
She's a young thing and cannot leave her mother.

Shuckin' of the Corn

Words and music traditional

I have a ship on the o - cean, - - - all lined with

sil - ver and gold. - - - Be - fore I'd see my true love

suf - fer, that ship should be an - chored and sold. - - - I'm a -

go - in' to the shuck - in' of the corn, - - - - I'm a - go - in' to the (chorus)

shuck - in' of the corn, - - - a - shuck - in' of the corn and a - blow - in' of the

horn, I'm a - go - in' to the shuck - in' of the corn.

The wind blows cold in Cairo,
The sun refuses to shine.
Before I'd see my true love suffer,
I'd work all the summer time.

(repeat chorus)

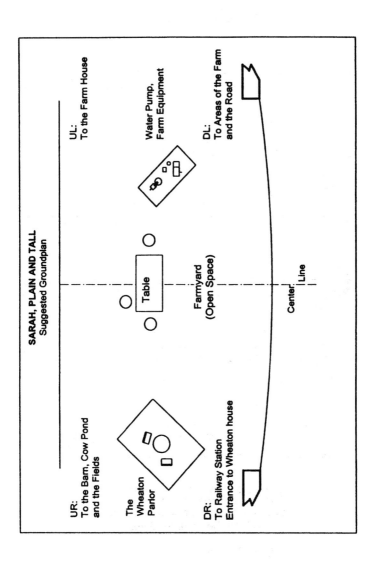

SARAH, PLAIN AND TALL
Suggested Groundplan

UL:
To the Farm House

Water Pump,
Farm Equipment

DL:
To Areas of the Farm
and the Road

Table

Farmyard
(Open Space)

Center
Line

UR:
To the Barn, Cow Pond
and the Fields

The
Wheaton
Parlor

DR:
To Railway Station
Entrance to Wheaton house

DIRECTOR'S NOTES

DIRECTOR'S NOTES

DIRECTOR'S NOTES

DIRECTOR'S NOTES

DIRECTOR'S NOTES